THE
Last
Good KISS

JANICE PINNOCK

THE Last Good KISS

SBI

STREBOR BOOKS

NEW YORK LONDON TORONTO SYDNEY

Strebor Books
P.O. Box 6505
Largo, MD 20792
http://www.streborbooks.com

ISBN-13 978-1-59309-055-5
ISBN-10   1-59309-055-2
LCCN 2008929334

Cover design: © www.mariondesigns.com

First Strebor Books trade paperback edition August 2008

10 9 8 7 6 5 4 3 2 1

Manufactured in the United States of America

For information regarding special discounts for bulk purchases, please contact Simon & Schuster Special Sales at 1-800-456-6798 or business@simonandschuster.com

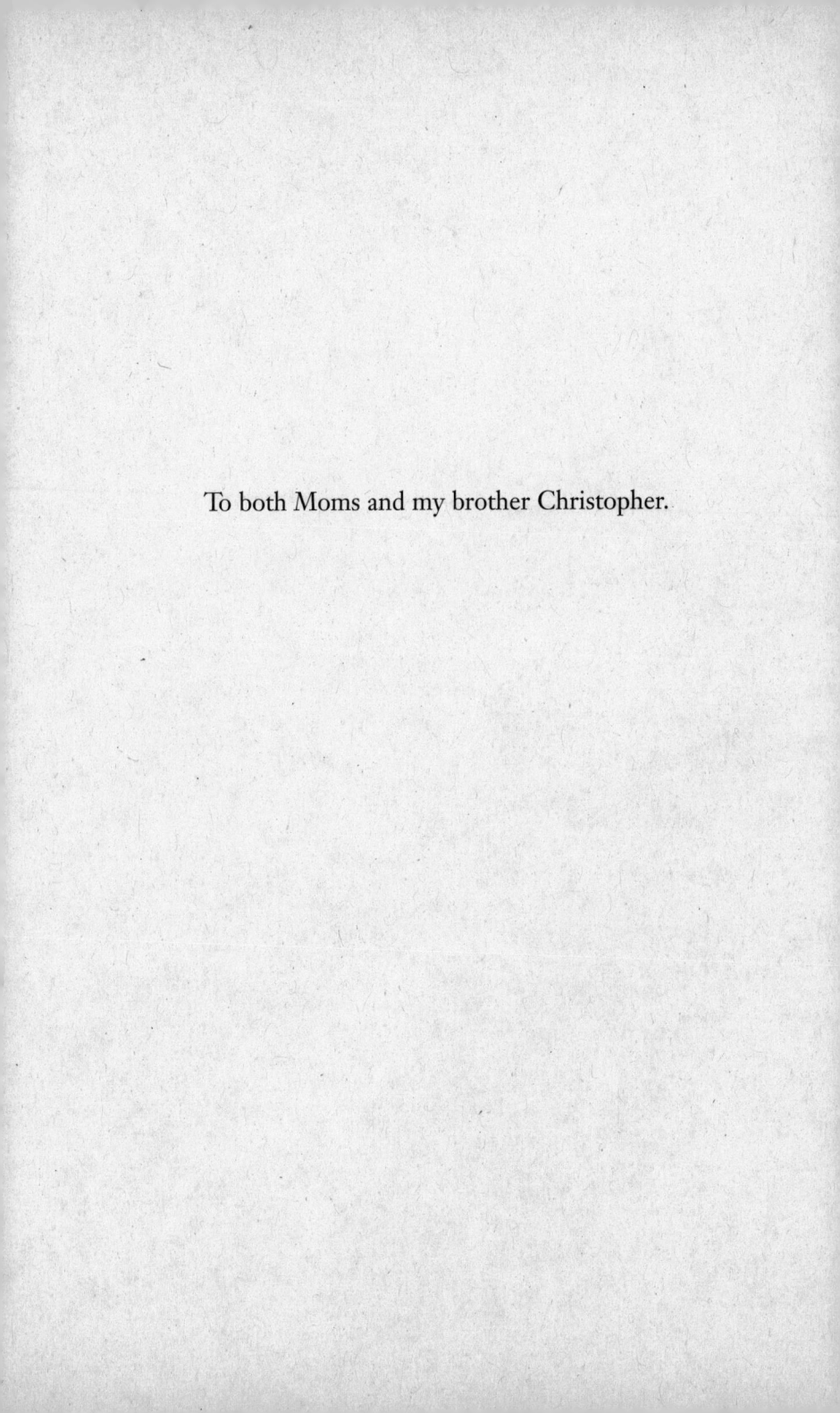

To both Moms and my brother Christopher.

Acknowledgments

I am first and foremost indebted to Franklin White for reading a poorly executed short story I had on the internet. He saw something in my writing I hadn't known existed. Thank you for having faith in my writing; it has made all the difference.

I would also like to thank Strebor for continuing to take on this book despite the obstacles and challenges.

Dedication

For you,
I don't know how to tell you
The things deep in my heart.
I don't even know if I should.
I can't form the words that are inside my head.
I don't know if I could.
There's so much that I want to say.
But all these thoughts just get in the way.
For you are my love, my heart.
I can't help but feel like I've fallen in love
in a moment, in a dream, on a whim
All I know is I want you near,
Forever, for always. May our love never dim.
It hurts to see the look in your eyes
I need you, you need me, I speak no lies
For you are my love. You are my heart.

Author's Foreword

It took me one month to write the first manuscript of this book. It then took me about one week to make my first changes. In its first publication, there was something that was missing from this book. What was missing was *my* connection to it. I have often said, a book is like your baby. You spend countless hours trying to bring it up right. In the end all you can do is hold your breath and hope that when you release it out into the world it is strong enough to stand up on its own.

The first manuscript I released without *"bringing it up right."* In this second version, I prayed for the wisdom to write something I could connect with. Here, I finally feel that I have done that. It is only through God's divine grace that saw me through an *entire year* of changes. I made up people, and places, buildings, and words. I even played with some of the things we consider to already exist. In other words, please do not look to this book for accuracies. What I would hope that you look to this book for is enjoyment, a touch of wisdom, and hopefully, a little bit of love.

Janice Pinnock
Bucheon, South Korea
December 2007

To My Restrained Love

I sat so still trying hard to breathe
My hairs stood up like bars of steel
I wonder why, but dare not think,
Had I let an angel pass, because I was so blind?

I reminisce the past in my pool of tears,
I remember the times I could've been your king
The wonder of your love has not left my soul,
I cleave to the taste of our first kiss.

My hands are bound, but my soul is free
My love is here and I know it's well
Love will fight to set you free
From the restraints that act as your heart's hell.

The tempest rises, the mountains melt,
The storm has raged, the wind has blown
The birds are stunned but have to sing,
Those restraints cannot hide you from what I've always known.

One more thing before I hold my peace,
our souls respond to each other's cries
Let me say it before I stop the ink
Your love yearns for me in the dungeon, behind your eyes

Your Patient Lover

Prologue

So he's writing a novel. Up until this point, I have not written any-thing longer than a grocery list. But, there is one thing that I firmly believe: When I put my mind to something, it's going to get done. So, I'm going to write a "story."

"Margo, come down from there," I am yelling. I can see her hanging from the banister and trying to kick her pudgy little legs over. She stops what she is doing guiltily, and plops her behind down on the stair. She smiles at me in that "don't be mad at me, I'm too cute" way, and I cannot help but laugh at her.

So I want to tell you about my friends, my family, and my life, just because I figure it's an inspiring story, or something like it. Who knows, maybe even Oprah-worthy? Yes, this coming from someone whose grocery list is usually cut in half, because she's tired of writing. Don't get me started.

Here we go. Enjoy!

One

one year earlier…

The look on his face betrayed his message before he even sat down. I knew that he was deliberately avoiding my questioning gaze. I was desperate for good news and he knew it. Yet, there was going to be none of that today. My palms suddenly felt cold and clammy, and the pit of my stomach felt as though it had a sack of bricks dropped directly into it. I gripped the chair, fearing my sudden dizziness might cause me to fall over. Finally, I looked at my mother and marveled at her composure. It was something that I had tried to mimic since I was a little girl. Looking at her proud, self-assured frame made me want to cry instead of sit up straight and play composed. If he was about to tell us that the cancer in her breast was as serious as he had originally thought, I didn't know if she would even be here to sit so straight much longer.

"Zora. How are you?" he asked.

She silenced him with a steely and direct gaze. "Cut to the chase, buster. What's the deal?"

"I'm sorry," he began. The rest blurred in my head. I felt as though my eardrums were on fire, and his words were slowly seeping out onto my shoulders. My breath caught in my throat and I fought hard to control the tears. He was sorry that she was going to die.

"...thirty percent of one breast...into the lymph nodes. Immediate admittance and surgery is necessary...," he continued.

"Are you certain?" I heard myself whisper. My voice came out sounding foreign and strange. Finally, he looked at me with sad, apologetic eyes. I pulled my gaze from his, and finally let the tears come. They dripped down my face, and dampened my lap. I imagined they might never stop falling. I was even more embarrassed when my mother stood up and pulled me to my feet. She embraced my much smaller body, and tucked me into that protective shroud her body provided. It had comforted me when I was small, and the realization that it might not always be there to comfort me, gripped my heart and shred it into a million little pieces. I cried hard on her shoulder because I missed her already and she was still here. I cried because she was comforting me when she was the one that had to deal with the possibility of death.

Two

My father used to tell my mother that she looked like a white woman with black skin. I guess he considered this a compliment. My father had always loved white women. His twin brother, Tony, wouldn't date white women. He said they were "way too fertile."

When I was eight, my mother says I had a meltdown. I developed an ulcer, and stayed in the hospital two weeks. I remember Mom kept telling me I had to learn not to worry and not to stress. She told me I was too young to stress. I remember waking up in cold sweats in that hospital room, my gut hurting as I worked myself into yet another meltdown. The doctor wanted to know why I might be so stressed. He said our focus was to relieve some of that stress. That was what would cure my ulcer. His eyes bore into mine, patiently waiting for me to talk. He wanted a tear or a small clue that I was a little girl just dying to tell my secret. But, my lips were sealed. I had broken his gaze and looked at my mom. She, in turn, looked away from me. Her face was riddled with shame and hurt. I imitated my mother's silence.

It wasn't until my dad's sister, Aunt Marie, came to visit that my life changed.

"Tammy, baby, you have to know that your father's behavior is not a result of anything to do with you. It is not your fault that he is a dog. You need to remember that. Sugar, you need to stop stressing yourself. You and your mother are better off without my brother. You hear? You done made yourself sick and it be tearin' up your insides." As she spoke, the pain in my gut had returned, and after about five minutes of talking, she noticed that my face was scrunched up in pain. She called the nurse.

Later that night she and Mom got into an argument in the hallway. Mom wanted to know what she had said to make me so upset.

Aunt Marie told her plain as day, "Zora, you better change those locks on your door. Do not let that man back into your house. He will kill you. The Lord sent me here today to tell you that. If you don't listen, he will kill you, and maybe that baby in there, too."

Two days later Mom sat on my bed stroking my head. "He's not coming back, okay?" she whispered. "No more fights, no more arguments. No more hitting. No more breaking of things. So you stop worrying, okay?"

I remember looking at her as though we shared a very private bond. She was mine, and I was hers. I nodded slowly. Then, just before tears sprang to her eyes, she stood up and walked out of the room.

A month after I had been released from the hospital, I was on the porch cleaning my imaginary kitchen with the little girl across the street. A beaten-up hunk-a-junk car pulled up to our curb, and screeched to a halt. My dad jumped out. And, without so much as a lingering glance in my direction, he went to the corner of the yard. Garbage bags, full of his clothes, had been rained on, and burnt by the hot sun. A stray dog had peed on them. He picked up the bags, and walked back down the path to his car without turning back. That was how he left my mother. That was how he left me.

I used to sit on my bed staring at a picture of my mother when she was twenty-one. She looked like a model. It was a mesmerizing picture of her caught off guard in her front yard. Her long hair was lifted by the wind, as she turned around to tell the person not to take the picture. Her face spread into a pretty, playful smile. Her lips covered a perfect set of straight white teeth. My mother has this natural beauty that captivates people—me included. I would sit and wonder how anyone could leave my mother.

When I was a teenager, I used to cry myself to sleep sometimes. I was convinced that I would be lonely and sad forever. If a man could leave a woman as beautiful as my mother, then surely one would leave me. I felt I paled in comparison to my mother. I used to stare at her for hours, and mimic her movements, her speech and her mannerisms. Sure, most children imitate their parents, but I grew to learn that a lot of people imitated my mother. She had that certain something that people wanted to imitate.

My grandmother on my mother's side is Swedish. She has stereotypical blonde hair and blue eyes. My granddad was from Barbados, which makes for an interesting mix in my mother. My mother is the kind of beautiful that causes accidents.

When I was about fifteen, I once let it slip that I wanted to be just like her. She had been putting on her stockings for church. She turned to me on her bed, and stared me straight in the face.

"Why?" she had asked.

"Because. You're beautiful. And, you get to be white and black. All the pretty girls at school are mixed," I told her. Her face scrunched up into a pained expression.

"You be proud of who you are. Regardless of whether you have a dime in your pocket, or a grand in the bank. Whether you have blue eyes or you're black as night. Be happy to be Tamara Jones. God made you who you are. That is perfect! There will never be another person like you. You hear me?" When I didn't answer, she looked me square in the eyes, and asked me again. Finally, I nodded.

My mother lived with her parents in Barbados until she was sixteen, and then moved to Jamaica to live with her aunt. That's where she met my father, Webster Jones. He came from a long line of mechanics, which is a commendable occupation in Jamaica. At first my mother's aunts didn't want them to speak. My father was apparently from the wrong side of the tracks. However, based on his occupation, my mother's aunts allowed them to see each other. My mother claims Daddy had already fallen madly in love with her, and had been busy planning how he would kidnap her from them regardless. My parents dated for a year and then moved to New York. They married a few months after arriving. I was born two years later.

I closed the door of my apartment, my feet aching, my knees sore and my back out of sorts. The minute I kicked off my shoes, and set my briefcase down on the floor, I dragged my feet across the shiny hardwood floor. I pulled my hair down, took my earrings off and unbuttoned my blouse. I was so tired, I briefly entertained the idea of sleeping right there on the couch. I pressed the message button on my machine and walked to the fridge to get a glass of water.

"*Tami, it's Dev. I'm in Manchester. I'll call you when I get to Portugal next week. Love ya, babe! Bye!*"

Devora has been one of my closest friends since grade school. She is a travel agent, and her *husband-neglecting* ass now travels around the world three-hundred days a year.

"*Tamara.*" Pause. "*Where are you, child?*" Pause. "*It's nearly five o'clock.*" Pause. "*Call me when you get in.*" Pause. "*Love you...bye!*"

That's my mom. She hates machines, but I think she hates the idea of me living so far from her even more.

The next message was the one that I had been waiting to hear all day. "*Hi, Baby, it's me. How do you feel about a late dinner tonight? I know I saw you last night, but I miss you already. I'm still at work. Call me on my mobile...Bye, Baby*"

That's Tyrone Livingston. He is the man of my dreams. I closed my eyes one night after a particularly horrible date, and prayed. I asked God to send me a man that I wouldn't have to someday daydream about killing in his sleep. I was lucky to have Ty, the man of my dreams, be the man in my bed. Tyrone was a damn good catch. I know that from the bottom of my heart. I wanted his hands on my back, and kneading my calves. He had magic fingers, I swear. I wanted to drape myself across his chest and just fall asleep. Or maybe his back, so I could rub up on his booty. Let me tell you, built like a house. And, skills like nobody's business. But, I can't share that. It would be X-rated material. Well, maybe just a little—delicious lips. He is intelligent, he's successful, he runs an electrical engineering company, owns more than one sexy car, and rents a condo in Westfalls. He was the epitome of every woman's dream. He didn't have to ask me if we could have a late dinner. He could come over and read me the recipe on a box of cereal, never cook a damn thing and I would swear it was the best evening ever. His presence was *that* fulfilling.

I flopped down on the couch and let out a sigh of relief. Every day should be Friday. I flicked the stereo on. Donnell Jones was on the turntable, where he and D'Angelo had been alternating roles for the past month. Okay, so I'm a bit of a routinist. It works for me! Donnell has a voice like honey: smooth, soft and sweet. Not to mention the man has some serious lyrical talent as well. Yes! Donnell, I will marry you. And, it's alright, too. We have the same last name, Baby.

It was almost six when I finally reached for the phone and dialed Tyrone's cell phone. He answered right away in that deep, smoldering sexy voice. I loved that. I took a moment to breathe in deeply as if savoring the sound of his voice.

"It's me," I said finally.

"I was just thinking of calling your cell phone, baby," he said.

"I just got in. I had some things to finish up," I replied, groaning a little. I stretched my long legs all the way down the length of the couch, and rested my arm on my stomach. It lurched. I was starved.

"Are you okay?" I don't know why I got butterflies when he asked me that question. I mean it's an everyday question, right? But when he asked I always felt as though he really cared. I couldn't help but feel warm inside.

"Mmm-hmm…how was your day?"

"Fabulous now. You up for dinner?"

"Depends what you have in mind," I whispered.

"Hmm…dinner at Chez Tyrone's. I hear they've got great after-dinner action," he replied.

I laughed out loud. Priceless!

"What's on the menu?"

"Tamara a là carte."

I burst into laughter yet again. I liked that idea even better. All the girls knew that Tyrone was the most amazing man I had ever been with. It's strange because I had never once mentioned a word of his...okay! Well...maybe I had. But I mean I didn't give them details. Okay...so maybe I'd mentioned some. Oh! Who the hell was I kidding? Once a month the girls and I sat down at one another's place, and gabbed about our boyfriends, our husbands, our exes, our bosses. You name it, and it was on the agenda. The one rule: No men are allowed. Even if he were president of the United States, he doesn't get access to our group. All eight of us went to high school together and had been inseparable through marriages, college, babies, and moves. In fact, we had grown closer.

I was pulled from my thoughts as he said, "Gorgeous, I'll see you around eight-thirty then."

"Sounds good. I'll see you later."

Ty and I had been dating for the better part of nine months. So far it had been right out of a dream. All my life I had worn my heart on my sleeve, only to have it stomped on. Or someone *accidentally* spilled burning hot coffee on it. I mean, I could move on, but I'd always have those scars. I just had to fight against it consuming me.

Ty had to be different.

I'd had my healthy share of boys and men. Sometimes you can't distinguish between the two, until they go and do something utterly ridiculous. You realized they were children. You had to shake your head, and say, *Good job, you done screwed it up real good! Get lost!* I am by no means a woman to be had. No man or boyfriend has every "owned me." Don't believe me, ask Dalyle. He had a busted nose when I was done with him. But that's another story for another time. Rule number one: I am independent. I'd rather have a split personality than have a man run my life. I have other rules, but for the most part, I make them up as I go.

Although I did not live in Westfalls, I didn't consider myself any less fortunate. I lived in Providence. I had my own penthouse apartment on the twelfth floor of a nice building. I worked at Bronx West Global as the financial manager. I took care of the day-to-day operations of all the company's finances. I dealt with the pay for celebrities like Mel Gibson and Nicolas Cage, right down to the girl in the mailroom. I had two degrees, one in international business and relations, and another in internal financial management. I had never been convicted of a crime, never been pregnant, never been hungry. I had been smart all my life, and beautiful, too. I couldn't complain about my thighs, or lines on my face, or extra meat on my butt, because I looked damn good. I curved where I should, and in some places that I shouldn't, but there wasn't a man that could keep his eyes off me. And this I know from years of having low self-esteem. From years of fighting with my hips, and my laugh lines, and whatever else *I thought* was wrong with me. I got this way from dealing with men who got off in bathrooms, while having dinner with me. I got this way from boys who made me feel as though their failures were mine. I used to cry for hours wondering how the hell to get a guy, and then ended up in tears, because I couldn't figure out how the hell to get rid of him. I was sick of crying because men I loved failed to love me back, or failed to love me right. Essentially, I got this way from going through what women all over the world go through every day of their lives.

Then one day, I stopped. I looked in the mirror and saw a beautiful person. I remembered Mom telling me God made me beautiful. The minute I realized that, I stopped judging myself by the way I *thought* people saw me. My life suddenly became easier. I had never had a lack of dates, just a lack of good choices. Losing myself was a dark, disgusting period of my life. Then I had it back. I suddenly didn't care if I seemed stuck up, and occasionally overconfident. I was working it, and then some!

Three

One thing that I am the first to admit is I do not have patience. I can't stand waiting, and I can't stand suspense. I stood on Ty's doorstep ringing his bell to no avail. A young man sat on the stoop next door strumming away on a guitar. He looked at me as though he was writing a song for me. He kept licking his lips in a purely sexual fashion, and I thought I might throw up. Just as I pulled my phone out of my purse, and was about to turn around and head back to my car, I felt an arm on my back. I spun around ready to knock someone out with my purse. Tyrone began to laugh deeply as I gave him my very best, unimpressed look.

"They just let anyone into this neighborhood?" I asked.

He raised a brown paper bag toward me, and smiled in a *please forgive me* sort of way.

I grunted.

"Open it!" he said excitedly. "It's a peace offering."

I took the bag from him, and smelled. It was a lot like something I had been craving for the past month or so. I was supposed to be on detox. Patties were out of the equation.

"Are these Jamaican patties, Tyrone?"

"Perhaps." He smirked.

I couldn't even look at them; I would insist on eating every single one. I suddenly began to think of the flaky brown pastry that seemed to just melt in your mouth. The way each bite crumbled and tasted on your tongue. Oh God, and then the spices, the meat, and the pepper. The smell and the…I was already ripping open the bag to take a look. "You know I can't have these."

"If I remember correctly, the rule was that *you* couldn't buy them."

"Yes. I guess technically I didn't buy them." I slumped down to the step. He sat beside me as I reached into the bag, and held out the delectable treat. Jamaican patties were my ultimate weakness. I was going to savor it. As I was just about to take a bite, I looked at my boyfriend, who looked at me. In a purely loving gesture, I held up the patty to let him take the first bite. He smiled slowly, in a pleased sort of way. He took my hand in one hand, tore off a piece of patty with the other, and then held the piece to my mouth.

"You deserve it," he told me. As I ate, I smiled at him wondering if anyone on Earth had ever known me better than him.

"Is this dinner?" I asked.

He laughed heartily. "Actually, no, I was cooking and thought I bet you'd love this for an appetizer, and ran down the street."

"You're so good to me, you know that?"

"Not nearly as good as you are to me!"

For a moment we both had nothing to say. He leaned forward and took a bite of the half-eaten patty in my hand. Then he stared at me, as I stared at him, both of us chewing and thinking. I knew he was the one. I just knew. The sun had started to set, the streetlights had just come on, and save for a few sprinklers and a lone child playing a few doors down, it seemed eerily quiet. Then, a soft tune echoed from the guitarist sitting on his stoop. A soft and beautiful ballad that I couldn't name, yet seemed to sum up my feelings.

Four

I have seven of the most beautiful, intelligent, sexy, funny, artistic, sensible, but unfortunately confused women as my close friends. Daeshondra Wallace, Jaclyn Thomas, Olivia Banks, Precious Rollins, Shaquonda Brown, Traci Williams and Devora Charles are the sisters that my mother did not give me through birth.

Daeshondra, also known as Dae, and I used to run track together in high school. Daeshondra is the funny one. Her life and her mentality are so backward. Although Daeshondra is the oldest of us all, she acts as though she is twenty-nine backin' the truck up to fifteen. She is still a virgin, still lives at home with her parents, and has a five-month rule. FIVE! When dating, there is to be no kissing before the fifth month. This, of course, should explain her virgin status. She is usually single, and thus we all determined her days of sexual frustration will indefinitely last forever.

Jaclyn is the most beautiful. She had been the nerdy, awkward, too tall, too skinny one in high school. But then Jaclyn found beauty magazines, and literally became one of the most beautiful models in the world. I'm not exaggerating. She modeled for Elite Models Inc. What is strange, however, is that the pictures that the girls and I see in the magazines make Jaclyn look so sweet and innocent. We all know the truth: Jaclyn is a whore in disguise. At last check this girl had at least forty-five men on her sexual conquest list. This, she revealed to us during a "circle of trust." Actually, she was drunk out her damn tree and started flapping her mouth a little too much. She still had enough sense to call for a circle of trust, though. This circle has existed between us girls since the ninth grade. It simply states that if one of us discloses any sort of private information after calling a circle of trust, it can never be discussed or brought up again without the person who discloses initiating it. I, for one, was dying to talk about it afterward.

Olivia, often referred to as Liv, is the sensible one. Liv often appears quiet, modest and shy. But, she is the one that taught us how to kiss, taught us how to flirt, and introduced us to boys. Liv is also driven by money and success. You don't want to compete with Liv for a job, a position or a prize. And, if there is anyone you best keep away from your man it is Liv. Liv has a four-year-old boy that she is raising on her own. His father, Brick, used to go to school with us. He always ran with the wrong crowd, however. After high school he got mixed up with the *worst* of the wrong people and has been frequenting rehab.

Precious is the most intelligent of us all. Precious knows the answer to all the *Jeopardy* questions. We can never play any trivia board games with Precious, because we don't have a hope in hell. All her life Precious has done everything her mother, God, her teachers, her friends, her grandmother and even strangers have told her to do. However, despite all the sense she has, she is also the one who can't say yes to closing her legs. Precious got pregnant and married at nineteen. Her husband was a useless tit. They have managed to produce four children, and have yet another one in the oven. The children take after Precious, however, and have more sense than their father. Apparently, contraceptives are a foreign word in the Rollins house.

Shan is the sexy one. She has one of those typical ghetto names that I just cannot stand. I was the one who coined the nickname Shan to make her a name a little more tolerable. Shan has four failed engagements behind her, and has not been in a single relationship in two years. The first fiancé went skiing in Alaska with his best guy friends a month before the wedding. He called Shan before the trip was even over, telling her he thought one of his "boys" excited him more than she did. The second fiancé couldn't deal with the fact that Shan made more money than him. While they were at Bergdorf's picking out dishes, they argued about how much they should spend on the plates. He worked himself into such a huff and puff that he walked out and never looked back. The third fiancé tried to use Shan for a punching bag, at which point she pulled a knife on him and told him to get the hell out of her damn house. I actually thought the fourth fiancé had some hope. Then he decided he wanted to convert to narcissism and told Shan he was too good for her. So, Shan is still looking, and last I had heard is entertaining the idea of dating her gynecologist.

Traci is going to be a world-renowned artist someday. I'm certain of it. When we were younger, Traci was the rebel in our group. She got a tattoo on her ankle. She pierced her nose and her tongue by herself. Traci cut her hair off to a low afro to protest the way black women were marketed on television. She introduced us to yoga, on her living room floor. She farted a little to encourage us to get in touch with our bodies, and get comfortable with one another's. Traci is also a single mother and has a little girl named Rochelle that she is raising on her own. Traci writes, paints, draws, sings, and invents. Sometimes she will come up with these random ideas that none of us can follow because they are beyond any of our comprehension. Right now she is dating some Canadian guy that she sees only once a month, but he does all right by her, so we can't complain.

Last is Devora. Devora is confused. Devora appears to always be stuck between a rock and a hard place. She and I used to be the closest. Her travel schedule is out of control these days, however. She finished flight attendant training about three years ago, and since that point has been working like a mad woman. I know for a fact that she put her name in for extra flights, although she denies it to everyone else. I believe she really wanted to get a divorce the day after she got married, but was too damn scared to ask for one. I also think she's waiting for him to leave her. She occasionally acts like she loves him, though. Who knows with that girl? Devora is the most noncommittal individual I know. Yet she is loyal. In a circle of trust I admitted I would touch Devora's body. But, if you saw her body, you'd want to touch it, too. That girl ain't playin' when it comes to being fit.

We have been there for one another the way that no one else in my life has ever been. Their loyalty rivals that of the love I receive from my mother. It is fundamentally different, however. I'd never go to my mother for advice about sex; that's what girlfriends are for. When I really sit down and think about it, these women are my sisters through and through.

Five

I was sitting in my mother's kitchen. She was cooking curried chicken and rice. I often wished that her cooking skills could be soaked into my brain through osmosis. Yet, none of that had happened just yet. Precious told me once that men rarely know how to cook. She said if I didn't learn my children would be eating canned soup and TV dinners. I generally just do not have the patience to sit and listen to Mom talk about what goes where and when. Throwing it all into the pot at once makes the most sense to me.

"Miss Dee's not well," Mom said suddenly. I looked up from the onion I had been tasked to cut. Miss Dee was her next-door neighbor. For as long as I could remember, Mom and Miss Dee have been spending summer evenings on the porch, talking about the old days. They became a lot closer after Mom kicked Dad out. Miss Dee was also a single parent. She had two boys. The youngest was Quincy, also known as Q.

Quincy Baker was the basketball star at Alexander Hamilton High. Her older son, Jamil, was in a penitentiary somewhere upstate. No one appears to know why. The boys had different fathers. Miss Dee always said Jamil took after his father who was shot in a gang war and died when Jamil was nine. A few years after his death, Miss Dee met Quincy's father, Heathcliff. Miss Dee always said, *"He frigged off and left,"* when he found out she was pregnant. As far as I knew, Quincy had never met his father.

Quincy was born a few months before me. My mother, who was pregnant with me at the time, stood next to Miss Dee during her delivery and helped Miss Dee bring Quincy into this world. I really didn't have much choice but to be friends with Quincy, but that happens when you spend most of your waking moments together. Most little girls don't like boys, but I never really thought of Quincy as a boy, unless he jacked with one of my Barbies. I remember when he cut off Malibu Barbie's long black hair, telling me she would look better. Then there was the time he burnt Barbie's dream house right down to the pink and melted brown rubber. Mom beat him, and then Miss Dee beat him, too, for playing with fire. And the whole time I jumped up and down crying over my dream house, and then Mom beat my ass, too. That time I didn't speak to him for four whole hours.

Yes! Quincy and I went a long way back. It wasn't until junior high that we kind of went our separate ways. I was popular and so was he. I was a bookworm and he was a troublemaker and the class clown. He played basketball. I ran track. We were probably too different to remain friends, but I don't remember particularly caring. I do remember the girls at school asking questions about him, and me acting as though I hardly knew him. I acted like we hadn't been bathed in the same tub for the first three years of our lives. I acted like we didn't have ties near close as blood. In the sixth grade we didn't walk together anymore. Our friends would come and meet us to walk to school. He and his friends walked on one side of the road and my friends and I on the other. But I guess that's what happens when you grow up. Or grow apart.

It was in eleventh grade when we finally noticed each other again. Don't get me wrong; I knew he was there. He knew I was still next door, and sometimes we'd still shoot some hoops, or he'd come over and ask for stuff for his mother, and talk to me. But, we weren't like we were back then. In the eleventh grade, I was a track star, he was the basketball star, and he came over for some sugar. Mom was out, and I was in the kitchen, doing some homework. He came through the door looking like he was just in a bar fight. His eye was black and swollen. I smirked. Good old Quincy. I was wearing a bandage on my wrist from a fall. As I was pouring him a cup of sugar, he started pissing me off.

"How in hell do you get injured playing some stupid sport like track? Or hurdles, or whatever the hell you were doing?" He said it purely disinterested, but it irked me more than I could explain.

"Why you gotta call it a 'stupid' sport, Quincy? It takes a hell of a lot more stamina than basketball. Now that's a dumb sport! It ain't like the hoop's goin' anywhere, but everyone's running around trying to shoot into a stationary object. Y'all should sink every shot. You have enough practice on it. It's pure foolishness!"

"Man…you don't know nothing…"

"Don't know *anything*, Quincy Baker; that's a double negative," I snapped. I shoved the sugar into his chest which caught him off guard. The cup spilled to the floor. I gave him a dirty look, and bent to clean it up. After kissing his teeth, he got down on his hands and knees to help me clean it up. That's when he started being nice.

"You like Ryan Benjamin?" he asked. I hated the guy. He was an arrogant jock, who had a reputation for getting girls pregnant and bragging about it.

"He's garbage," I replied.

"He's been talkin' 'bout you in the change room. Somethin' 'bout you doin' stuff to him." By "stuff," I had known it was disgusting.

My mouth fell open and I stopped scooping the sugar and stared at him. What a jerk!

"That's how I got this!" He pointed to his eye.

I was overcome with feeling for the poor kid and reached up to touch his eye.

"Does it hurt?" I asked, and Quincy shook his head no.

He smiled a big broad, absolutely beautiful smile that seemed to belong only to us, and said, "I'm tough!"

Our first date was to the South Bronx Zoo. After that we were the buzz at school. He played ball, and got a scholarship to NYU. I was senior class president, valedictorian, and got a scholarship to NYU as well. But a high school basketball star rarely survives unless they also have academic drive. Despite what you see on TV, and read in books, they don't fly by with D's because they got ball skills. Well, not at NYU. Quincy didn't make it past the three-month probation period, and neither did our relationship. After he left NYU we didn't see each other or talk much, either. He began running around with a gang, and was arrested for some minor offenses, like driving with an invalid license, and writing bad checks, followed by a more serious burglary charge. I was soon convinced that I did not need Quincy in my life. Before him I had dated two boys, one right after the other. After we broke up, I dated too many to count—none of which were worth my time.

Mom suddenly interrupted my thoughts. "Are you listening?"

"Sorry. I'm daydreaming. What's the matter with Miss Dee?" I asked.

"Her blood pressure. The doctor said she's had two mini strokes. She needs to start eating healthy, and exercising. We both know that to Miss Dee, exercise is a foreign language."

"Maybe you two should start going for walks in the evening, Mom. Instead of sitting on the veranda, I mean."

"I failed to mention. It's a foreign language and a pain in the ass for me, too." She and I chuckled.

"How's Quincy?"

"The cops came again to get him this afternoon. It's a shame, you know? Quincy's a good boy. It's that no-good father of his. He's a terrible example for him. And not only that, but Dee is a good mother, even though that other boy of hers is trash. She doesn't need that."

I shook my head, and scraped the chopped onions into the pot.

"Not yet! You need to wait for the chicken to cook for a bit, or they're just gonna burn," she snapped, pulling the cutting board with the rest of the onions out of my hand.

"He needs someone to take him under their wing. That's what Quincy needs."

"I'm tired of everyone making excuses for Quincy. He is an adult. He can make his own decisions. Everyone wants to blame a bad man on a bad father."

"Who made you the judge?"

"I'm just sayin' that Quincy's first mistake was dropping out of school. I never forgave him for dropping out. Maybe he's punishing himself, too." I reached for the salt to pour into the pot, but she slapped my hand away.

"Tamara, not everyone has their heads on straight, you know that? Not everyone is as perfect as you are. Thank the Lord for blessing me with you, especially in this damn neighborhood," she said.

I laughed. Only my mother would say "bless" and "damn" in the same sentence. "If the cops came for Quincy, it is nobody's fault but Quincy's."

"You're a snob," she said with a smile.

Six

I loved my job. Every now and then I actually got to meet someone famous, or semi-famous. Once I met this guy who was an extra in a movie with Quentin Tarantino. Some stars make six figures for two days of work. Once, Jennifer Lopez got five figures for a two-minute cameo in a movie. I needed to become a movie star.

I was the last person to apply for the job, and the only one that they considered giving it to. This came from Ron Sallinger, the man who hired me. I had a great office on the thirtieth floor of the French Building, right in the heart of Rockland. It was a good fifteen-minute drive from Providence. I had large bay windows that overlooked the city. I made it a habit never to close my office door. I took the "open door" policy literally. There were about fifteen people that worked directly under me, and I answered to Ron, who well, doesn't answer to anyone. Ron had ten managers that worked for him in departments like production, shipping and delivery, finance, accounts receivable and human resources. On Mondays, Wednesdays, and Fridays we had team meetings where we all got together and talked shop. Mostly I turned up for the free sandwiches and coffee.

I started work each day around eight-thirty, and was usually greeted by my intern, Gabrielle. My day often began with me double-checking the paperwork from the day before. By ten I would go through signing paychecks because Glen came around to do the mail at eleven. Usually by lunchtime I was still on the phone with clients about pay, or their agents, or other departments. Afternoons, however, were always different. There were meetings, sales pitches, business drives or running out of the office to go down to one of the studios we own to see how things were running.

One particular Monday I was slightly stressed over the fact that somehow Tori, the new girl, had misplaced three hundred and five dollars—not a big amount considering our gross profit. However, it's difficult to find where she went wrong without going right over the paperwork and starting again. The phone rang on my desk, and it was my mother. She was supposed to be at a church group meeting.

"Why are you home?" I asked. I had my ear to the phone and was tapping away on my computer.

"I have things to do. You don't get to ask me that," she snapped. "How are you?"

"Fine! Thanks. How are you?"

"Good! Listen…Quincy's in trouble. Did you hear about the kid that got beat up and almost died over on the west side? I think it was in Duchess County. I think it was May seventeenth?"

"Yeah! The kid that was involved in the gang fight," I told her. I could imagine her nodding her head up and down.

"That's what they arrested him for. They think he beat that kid."

That's when I stopped typing. My hand had landed on four or five keys, and was now spitting out random letters onto the screen.

"Did you hear me?"

"Are you sure? That's such a serious offense. He's usually in for something petty. Didn't the news say attempted murder? They said it was premeditated, too," I said more to myself than to her.

"Miss Dee called me this morning from the jail."

"This has to be a joke," I insisted.

"Child, I raised you better than to question the things I say. I'm telling you like I heard it. Quincy is finally in for something serious. That ain't a joke if you ask me," she said quickly. Then with a hurried and unimpressed good-bye she hung up the phone.

For the remainder of the afternoon I attempted to concentrate on work, but it just wasn't in me. I hadn't spoken to Quincy in at least six months, yet it seemed like we had spoken to each other yesterday. I had stopped by my mother's to drop off some vegetables from Aunt Vy's garden. Quincy was getting into a black car. He had paused for a moment, then whistled as though he didn't recognize me.

"Hi, Q!" I said with a smile, and I genuinely meant it. It was good to see him, and I gave him a kiss on his cheek. He was still standing by the car. By this time the other passengers had leaned over to stare at me, and some were giving me the "get with you" eye. I ignored them.

"You look prettier than I remember," he said.

"Thanks, Quincy. You look good, too. Not as good as me, but you aight still."

"Ohhhhh, so it's like that now." His face broke into a wide mischievous smile. I still liked the way he smiled, and the way we could joke with each other. But Quincy was going nowhere and doing it fast. I remembered briefly the boy who had held my hand at the zoo. I remembered the sweet young man who had kissed me with shaky palms, and nervous lips at the movies. I also remembered the shy and gentle person who had taken my shirt off in his room on the last day of my virgin life. He still looked that way to me. Now he hardly seemed to possess any of those qualities. I had tried to help him once before, but he didn't care. He didn't wanna hear it. Traci had told me he didn't wanna hear me preach.

I had stepped back from his car, and said good-bye. I walked up to my mother's porch, and opened the door. I turned around to look behind me to see if he was still there. He stared at me as though things hadn't changed between us.

Now Quincy was in jail for a serious offense. How on Earth was he going to get himself out of this one?

Seven

Since Ty and I had been together, I had never felt the need to be elsewhere during one of our lovemaking sessions. It's not even fair to call it a session because it lasted from the moment we saw each other and well into the night. When he took off my clothes the following Saturday evening, I realized my heart just wasn't in it. He stopped twice, sensitive to my lack of interest. I kept thinking of Quincy. I could kick myself for caring so much, but I couldn't figure out how to stop caring. When Ty could take it no more he rolled over, and pulled me tightly into an embrace. Most men either conked out, or moved away. Not Tyrone. He pulled me in, and cuddled me until *I* fell asleep.

"What's wrong?" he asked.

"Nothing," I whispered, snuggling into the crook of his neck and his shoulder. He felt all warm and damp. I liked that musky mixture of sweat and sex that lingered on his body. I loved the way his hard muscled frame felt pressed up against me. He reminded me of a six-foot-six, hard, chocolate statue.

"Tell me what's on your mind, baby. What happened today that has you so wound up? I can feel stress dripping off of you."

"Sorry," I whispered. But I had no intention of telling him what was going on. "Why isn't there a channel one on TV?" I asked.

He laughed so loud and so deeply that I couldn't help but laugh, too. Tears came to his eyes. I loved that he let the tears run freely without wiping them away.

"That's what you were thinking about?"

"Yeah!"

"Guess I was pretty boring, huh?"

"God no! You are the best!" I replied.

He seemed pleased by this answer and began caressing my hand that rested on his chest.

Finally I fell asleep this way.

When I woke in the morning, he was gone. His smell lingered on the sheets. Comforted, I snuggled back into my sheets and fell right back to sleep.

I finally rolled out of bed at ten-thirty. I showered quickly and dressed. I was meeting my cousin, Angela, for lunch. I assumed we would eat at McDonald's because she was bringing Parys, her five-year-old daughter. I loved Angela like we were sisters. Her mother, Aunt Vy, was an old friend of my mother's from Barbados. Having spent a lot of time together when we were younger, Angela and I had just decided we should be cousins.

When I pulled up at her house, Parys came racing out of the yard. She jumped into my arms.

"Hi, Aunty," she squealed. She grabbed my face between her hands and gave me a fierce "I love you too much" kiss.

Aunt Vy waved to me from the doorway. "Hi, baby," she called to me. I propped Parys onto my hip, and waved back.

"Hi, Aunt Vy. How were those flowers?" I asked.

"They were beautiful, Sugar. Thank you. Stop by when you come back. I've got some goat on the stove. It's gon' burn," she called.

Aunt Vy could cook like nobody's business, but she was so busy gossiping or on the phone that she burned ninety percent of the meals she cooked.

Angela ran out and enveloped me in a quick embrace.

"Hi, Handjobjula," I said, chuckling. I had called her by that nickname for years.

"Yo!" she exclaimed, and I smiled. She and Parys were spitting images of each other. They had dark heart-shaped faces and thick tight curls. They both had dark mesmerizing almond-shaped eyes. Parys, however, would someday be even more beautiful than her mother.

I opened the doors with my remote and then buckled Parys into her seat as Angela climbed into the car.

"Where are we going?" I asked Angela.

Three little boys on their bikes were riding past us on the street, and one of them yelled to me. "Nice car, Miss." I smiled. I guess my car does look out of place in this area. It wasn't the ghetto, but it wasn't too far from being one.

"Burger King," Angela replied, and then laughed.

"How about a real restaurant for a change?" I asked as I slid into my seat and buckled up.

"What about this one?" she asked, gesturing toward Parys in the backseat. Parys looked up at us a little confused as to why both of us were looking over the back of our seats at her. She chuckled. She was so damn cute. Angela had done her hair in pigtails, with colorful bobbles on them. She had dressed her in a cute, little red OshKosh sundress and put red sparkly studs in her ears. I squeezed her leg, and she giggled shyly.

"Parys is willing to eat whatever we eat," I told Angela. Parys nodded at us both. When I turned around, the kids on their bikes were in front of my car, still admiring.

"Hit 'em, they'll move," Angela said. She leaned out the window and yelled. "Levar, get out the street, before I tell yo momma where you at."

The three boys hopped on their bikes and rode furiously away.

"How about Windows on the World?" I suggested. I pulled away from the curb, and pressed the button to take the top off the car. It was such a beautiful day. It was the kind of hot you could stand because there was a strong breeze in the air. Parys squealed in the backseat and tried to push herself up to see over the body of the car.

"As long as they don't serve no frog legs. But damn if that ain't high class and expensive," she grumbled.

I gave her a dirty look, but laughed anyway.

When we pulled up to the parking lot, I realized how much I loved the place. It was high up on the 107th floor of the World Trade Center. It had this fabulous view of Manhattan, and a very retro atmosphere to it.

Conversation was easy and jovial at first, but all of a sudden, Angela became quiet. I looked between Angela and Parys. Parys sat at the end of the table by the window, playing with her mother's keys. Angela smiled at her, and then leaned in for a kiss, which Parys, like usual, returned fiercely.

"When I'm with you...I feel rich," Angela whispered. She glanced around, mesmerized by the atmosphere.

My heart was suddenly filled with sadness. She and I hadn't been all that different growing up. Our mothers had been close, and we had gone to the same school. Neither of us had fathers and our mothers had had comparable income. Yet her life had turned out so different. Sometimes I wished I could save her, and Parys. The problem, of course, was that I wasn't entirely sure how.

"Remember the interview I had for the translation job? I didn't go. There was a lice outbreak at her school, had to go get her at the last minute," she replied.

I sighed heavily. Angela worked as a dishwasher at Ryerson General Hospital. She barely made a penny above minimum wage. I had offered her a job at my office, but she insisted things might get awkward. In retrospect, I had to agree.

I noticed that Angela was nitpicking at her salad. When she noticed I was staring at her, she said, "Omar asked me to marry him."

Why in God's name had it taken her so long to tell me this?

Parys was eating a poutine—a mixture of cheese gravy and French fries all thrown together. Apparently that nasty-looking mess was a popular French dish. Angela had ordered a glass of milk to make her meal look semi-nutritious. Angela and I both ordered different fish dishes, which this restaurant was famous for. When she told me her Omar news, I choked on the fish I was chewing, and Parys spilled her milk in her plate.

"What did you tell him?"

"What do you think I friggin' told him?" She glanced over at Parys who now had her hands knuckle deep in gravy and looked as happy as a pig in shit.

"Well…I don't know, Angela. That's why I asked."

"What do you think I should have said?"

"I think, Angela…that you should have told him how you felt." I took a sip of my Perrier. Then instinctively I reached over and rescued Parys' elbow from the plate of mush.

"I just said I needed time. I guess because I am not one hundred percent sure…you know? I want Parys to have things. I want her to be someone. I want to move out of the freaking ghetto and live in upscale New York. Hell, I want to be someone," Angela spoke dreamily and then chuckled as though she'd had an epiphany. "Shit, Tamara, I wanna be you."

Eight

As I pulled up to my mother's, I saw her and Miss Dee sitting on the porch, sipping ginger beer. Miss Dee looked unhappy and haggard. Her mind must have been working overtime, with her two sons in jail.

"Beauty, you're looking good," Miss Dee said, and forced a smile. As I walked up the porch steps, I noticed her eyes were red and puffy. I knew she'd probably been crying since the police had taken Quincy away.

"How are you?" I asked her, and leaned over to kiss her cheek. I kneeled beside her and took her hands in mine. They were rough and dry. She had had such a tough life.

"Oh dear! I was better, but I went down there this morning. I saw him. He's putting up a front, but my baby's scared. I can see it in his eyes," she replied, and then dabbed at her eyes again. I had a hard time imagining Quincy scared of anything.

I turned to look at my mother. She looked down the street. This seemed to have taken a toll on her, too. I suddenly felt a pang of guilt for my entire generation.

"I don't think she should go see him," Mom piped up. I frowned.

"Zora, someone needs to. He can't just stay there alone," Miss Dee protested, and my mother kissed her teeth.

"Tamara will go! Won't you, honey?" And suddenly both of their steely brown eyes were glued on me.

"No! She doesn't have to do that," Miss Dee retorted.

But the look in both of their eyes told me I did. I couldn't say no. It would be wrong.

"I could go," I said.

Miss Dee searched my face for a betraying emotion, and when she found none, she pulled my face to hers, and kissed me. Her dry lips were surprisingly gentle on my cheek.

"Child, I love you like you were my own. You're a fine woman. Besides, you know Quincy loves you. He always has. You two should have gotten married. That was the plan right, Zora?"

"No one told me about any plan," Mom replied, but laughed regardless. "Admittedly, the dating plan did go as planned."

"You two knew we dated?" I asked.

Miss Dee adjusted her glasses on the top of her nose. "Oh! We knew…we knew *everything*, Tamara. Since you and he were tiny tots, biting each other in your playpen. Even during your senior year, when you two were bumpin' and grindin' in his bed."

I froze. What?

I looked over at my mother, who had a sly knowing smile on her face. She had known, too. And we had thought *we* were hiding shit. Crap!

"I'll go," I said, laughing as I went into the house. That was a cleverly planned out attack is what that was. They had dirt on me.

Mom swung her arm out and slapped my butt.

❤❤❤

I sat on the couch later that evening with a book in my lap, but my mind on Quincy. What would we say to each other? Would

I tell him how stupid he was for getting himself into trouble? Would we even have anything to say to each other? There was a knock on the door that interrupted my thoughts.

I opened the door to find a young woman with a basket of big, beautiful red roses. I looked on shocked. I knew they were from Ty before I signed for them. My heart leapt into my chest, and gave me that fulfilled feeling. It was like he was in my head—his senses acute to my wants and needs. After I put them in a vase in the living room I sat down to read the card.

> *Tami,*
> *I hope you've finally gotten the absence of channel one off your mind, and had a good day today.*
> *Miss you,*
> *Kisses,*
> *Ty*

I loved his scrawl. I loved that he knew I wasn't really thinking about channel one. Even as I sat smiling to myself, I was also sad. I wish he had said "Love, Ty."

I knew I was making too big a deal out of nothing. In fact, I hadn't said I loved him yet. More importantly I wasn't entirely sure I was in love with him. But I knew I wanted to be. He was the perfect kind of man to fall in love with. You know they say that every little girl dreams about Mr. Prince Charming, who would ride in on a horse and sweep her off her feet. I couldn't remember doing that. I just dreamt about a man that would be present, because my father never was. Ty had taught me the difference between a good man and a jerk. It was like I suddenly understood how that man riding in on the horse *should* behave. I'd never been the type of woman to play into the weakness of anybody, meaning women or men as the weaker sex. But, I did recognize what my concept of self, in relation to being a woman was. I knew what made me feel feminine, I knew how to play those things up, and I worked it every chance I got. I wanted to know that he was thinking about me when I wasn't around. If he took an extra second in his day to remind me of that, I'd do anything for him. It was holding my hand when we are walking down the street together. Not only did his actions say, "I'm proud to be with you," but they also say, "If you need some protection, I'm prepared for it." It was in the way that he listened to me. When I spoke, there was nothing else going on for him. He didn't interrupt, he asked the right questions, he got involved. He got excited about what I was excited about, or pissed off if I was. It was even in the way we were together. If we were in the same room, he made me feel desired, by reaching out to touch me. If we were at the movie theater, his hands were on my thigh, his fingers in my hair, or on my cheek. If we were in the elevator together, his arms were around me, and my space entirely invaded by him. And if we were alone in the elevator, there was an extreme makeout session, as if we had to get in as much loving in the shortest possible time. I guess what I'm remembering is the fact that he had this uncanny ability to remind me of the best things about being a woman, especially when I occasionally forgot.

Monday evening I decided to go see Quincy. All day I wondered if I would be able to hold my tongue and not give him shit. I hoped so. I worried about bringing something for him. Did they allow gifts for inmates? I'd never been to a jail before. In fact it hadn't been on my list of immediate things to do.

The Roosevelt Penitentiary is on Roosevelt Island, formerly Welfare Island and Blackwell Island. New York is spread out over a dozen islands. Long Island, Staten Island and Manhattan are the most famous. There is also Governor's Island and North and South Border Island.

It was a twenty-minute drive to the Bronx ferry and then a half hour for the ferry ride across to Roosevelt Island. I sighed. I was struggling with the fact that Quincy was there.

What was Barney Rubble's job? I thought suddenly. It kind of popped into my mind from nowhere, as thoughts often do. He had at least three jobs. He was once Fred's boss, when Mr. Slate had given him the job.

Roosevelt Island was home to loony bins and hospitals for years. I think it was Fred Gumble from *The New Yorker* who said Roosevelt Island was "used for society's undesirables." Although it sounds terrible, a rapist or a murderer is certainly undesirable to society. In the late 1800s they started housing victims of infectious diseases. Then I tried to list all the infectious diseases I could remember. I slammed on my horn as a man who was probably drunk attempted to cross the cars. He gave me the finger but backed up anyway. There's an infectious disease: road rage. I had no patience for road rage. I had other shit to take care of like coming up with infectious diseases: smallpox, typhus, cholera, tuberculosis, polio…I was at a loss for more.

My cell phone came to life, jerking me from my reverie.

"Hello," I said, while single-handedly maneuvering my way from behind a stalled car.

"It's me," Daeshondra said in her distinctly deep voice.

"What's up, Dae?"

"What does cum o sa va mean?" she asked. Despite her hideous attempt to translate, I did recognize it as a French greeting.

"How are you?" I replied.

"I'm fine...but...what does it mean?" she repeated.

I turned the car onto South Bronx Main Street. "Fool. The translation means, how are you." I laughed.

She began to laugh, too. "Where you goin'? I tried you at home."

"To see Quincy."

"That ass. Tell him I said hi. How is he, anyway?"

"In jail."

"Ouch! Well, maybe don't tell him I said hi. It might sound a little cruel!" she exclaimed. "What's he in for?"

"I don't know," I lied. I didn't want to say possibly attempted murder. People would forgive you for breaking and entering, they would forgive you for theft, and they might even forgive you for robbing them. But, they didn't like to associate themselves with murderers.

"Where are we meeting this month?" she asked, changing the subject.

"Traci's, I think. On the twenty-fifth." I pulled up to the ferry parking lot. I sat for another minute talking to her about nothing important. Finally, I said good-bye, and sat in the car waiting. Waiting—till I had to get on the ferry, and waiting for my pulse and my heart to stop racing.

Nine

I sat on the bench on the upper deck, attempting to look composed. But, inside I felt anything but put together. I was nervous and I was sad. I wasn't sure what I might find on the approaching island, or be it who. I wondered if Quincy was a different person than the boy I had grown up with. I hoped inside there were remnants of the boy that I had once loved. If he was a hardened criminal, I might be tempted to leave him right where he was.

Someone sat down about a foot away from me. I hardly noticed him, until his scent wafted into my nostrils. I inhaled deeply the sexy, musky odor mingling with the cool ocean air. I watched long enough to notice him opening *Great Dialogues of Plato*. I looked at him as though he had interrupted something very important. I turned my attention to the approaching Roosevelt Island. I'd found lately that I no longer looked at men the way I did when I was single. Maybe I no longer noticed them because I was in love. I hoped that was the reason.

On the drive to the jail, I had suddenly felt the need to call Ty. I needed to hear his voice. He picked up on the first ring, with excitement in his voice. He told me he was cooking shrimp pasta. Tyrone cooks almost as good as my mother. I could imagine him on national television, wearing a chef's hat and talking about sauces, and other exciting things that chefs talk about. When my mind stopped wandering, and I was reassured by his presence in my life, I promised him I would stop by later and got off the phone. I promised myself that this time, I wouldn't be anywhere else while we were making love. I would be in his arms. It was what he deserved, despite the turmoil that was going on in my life. I felt better. I was ready to do this. Quincy had been my friend for a long time, I didn't like the idea of seeing him behind bars, and I knew it would upset him if I let him know that. So, I gathered my composure and drove through the security gates.

As I reached the desk labeled VISITORS, I stood in line behind a vile-smelling, greasy young woman. She wore terrible shoes, and a dress that was entirely cut out in the back. It cut so low, I could see her underwear well above the hem. I held back a few feet as we stood there. I held my breath hoping that none of her stank would transfer itself on to me. When I finally reached the man behind the counter, he did a double-take. I tried hard not to notice, but he continued to stare at me as though he were looking through my clothes. I cast him a purely disgusted look and cleared my throat hoping to end this episode.

"I'm here to see Quincy Baker."

"Lucky fella!" he muttered.

"Excuse me?"

"Through those doors is a metal detector, and a guard. He'll search you and put your purse through a detector. Do not pass any objects to the prisoner. If you have any gifts for him, you need to declare them now," he told me. He then leaned over the counter and smiled crookedly at me.

I gave him a dirty look. "I have nothing to declare." I stared at him until he sat back down in his chair.

"Someone will come and get you when he's ready. Fill this out." He thrust a clipboard in my hand. I had to fill out my name, phone number, address, social security number and my relation to Quincy. I wrote "wife." Once I completed the form, I thrust the clipboard right back at him, and sat down. I took a seat. After waiting, and crossing and uncrossing my legs for what felt like an hour, I glanced at my watch. It had only been fifteen minutes. But then after twenty minutes, I began to worry. What if he had decided he didn't want to see me? I banished the thought from my mind. Why would he do that? He wouldn't. Finally, I heard them call my name. A female correctional officer beckoned me toward her. She was a short, stocky, black woman and about forty. She stood swinging a billy club. I averted my eyes as I approached her.

"This way, Miss," she said, and opened a door for me. Once I walked through, the door closed and then latched behind me. There were no bars, and no hard plastic windows. There was no two-way telephone like I had imagined. It was just a room. A twenty-by-twenty-foot room with a window. There was a table and two chairs. It was private. I felt relieved that Miss Dee hadn't had to see Quincy behind bars, or through plexiglass. I sat down on one of the chairs, and reflexively rapped my knuckles on the table. Then I stopped. A few minutes later I was shaking my crossed legs nervously. Then I stopped. At some point I realized I was biting my nails. I couldn't even remember the last time I had done that. When the door finally opened, Quincy walked in nonchalantly. He froze as he saw me sitting in front of him. Had they not told him who his visitor was? He looked surprised, then regretful.

Then there was relief or something like it, as he sat down opposite me. "Hi!"

Quincy had a fresh shave. His hair was buzzed, but he still

reminded me of Mekhi Phifer, even down to those big ole juicy lips. He was dressed in a gray uniform. It consisted of a loose-fitting T-shirt with a number on it, and a baggy pair of slacks.

"I didn't expect to see you here," he said. His gaze suddenly became challenging. He was letting me know that I didn't belong in a jail. That, I already knew.

"Well, you can thank yourself for me being here," I snapped.

He smiled. "Here we go. Still haven't changed. Still feisty."

"I don't plan on changing, Quincy."

For a moment there was silence. The only sound came from the guard turning his newspaper over as he sat by the door seemingly uninterested in our conversation.

He ignored my sudden burst of anger, and smiled at me again. "How have you been?"

"I'm all right. How are things in your new place?" I was painfully aware that every word coming from my lips was sarcastic and rude, but I couldn't stop myself.

He chuckled anyway. "Very funny."

For a moment I could see that scared look his mother was talking about. I felt scared for him. I wished there was something I could do.

"How's my mom?"

"She's a little sick. I think the buses, the subway and the ferry ride are a little taxing on her. So, I'm probably going to come see you from now on so she doesn't make the trip all the time."

"What's wrong with her?"

"Oh…nothing serious. Just tired."

"Oh! Okay. You don't have to come, you know," he stated.

"I want to," I answered, much too quickly.

And in a way I did want to see him. I could see for myself that he wasn't actually wasting away to nothing, and losing weight. I wanted to make sure fifty-year-old men with large tattoos were not trying to make him their wife.

"What happened, Quince?" I asked suddenly. I looked down at my hands. They were shaking. I was afraid for him in there. Jails just look like this on the outside, but I know on the other side there are rowdy dangerous men.

"You mean with us?"

I looked up at him, confused. What the fuck was that supposed to mean? "I mean…with this whole thing. Why are you wearing a gray Value Village shirt, with a freaking number on it? Why is your mother at home crying? What the hell happened?"

"It's a long story."

"Start talking then."

"Tamara, it doesn't concern you. Not to be rude, girl, I just don't want you to get involved. Just…just forget it," he said, exasperated.

Before I knew what I was doing, I smacked him upside the head.

He grabbed the side of his head and groaned. The guard looked over and smirked. Quincy looked at me as though I had wounded him. "Ouch!"

"Do I look like that dumb-ass ho you've been running around with?"

"No! Frigg…that hurt," he wailed.

"And by the way, has she come to see you?"

"No!" he snapped. "I don't even know if she knows. I didn't call her, and I don't intend to." He looked out toward the window. He always looked attractive to me.

"What happened, Quincy?"

"May seventeenth. Shoop, Trey, Zel, and me was rollin' downtown. Mindin' our own business. We had a gram or so. I wasn't smoking, though." He paused, looking at me as if to check whether or not I believed him. "Anyways, on Sixty-second Street, we run into a couple of guys from the Bloods. They was going to some party in Duchess County. We followed them down to Duchess. At this guy's crib, there's so much shit goin' on, it ain't funny. I was wonderin' where the cops were, man, 'cause the place was jumpin'. So, later a fight breaks out.

"Tami, I tell you I was there. I was inside during the fight. I watched some of it through the window. I thought they were just gonna rough him up a bit. But, I guess it was more than that. I didn't even see the worst part of the fight. I went back to the party. Then everyone started screaming the cops were there. Everyone started running. There must have been about fifty cop cars. I ran because everyone else ran. I didn't even know it was about the kid in the back. I just started running. I was looking for Zel and Shoop, out in the backyard. I didn't wanna leave without them, but I couldn't find them. In the backyard where they had beat the kid, people were running. There was blood everywhere. I kept looking around for Zel and Shoop. I guess it was the extra minute I took to find 'em. On my way over the fence, I felt myself going down. Some pig hit me on the head with his club, man. They took me to the shop, but released me that night. Then on the sixth, they came back telling me I dust that kid. I swear to you, I didn't do it. I wasn't even there for that shit."

"I believe you," I told him. He nodded as though my acceptance of his story was all he needed to hear. "Can you get anything in here?"

"Conjugal visits," he answered entirely too quickly and then laughed.

"Call your girl," I suggested.

"Nah! She ain't even worth it. She's gotta be hot, like you, so that the guards and all the man dem up in here will be jealous. They'll think Quincy got a hottie girl," he replied.

I laughed. But my laughter stuck in my throat as the seriousness off his situation suddenly dawned on me. I looked at him through worried eyes.

The smile melted from his mouth and he looked away. I fought back tears.

"I'm all right," he whispered, but still would not look at me.

"Who's your lawyer?"

"Some dread appointed by the feds," he exclaimed. "Bastard didn't even show up on time. In fact I've never even talked to him. Showed up at my prelim and didn't even say two words to me. Nigga's shit don't stink, I guess."

"Don't say that!"

"Sorry," he whispered.

"I'll go see him."

"Would you?" he asked, sounding vulnerable. "I wanna get out of here so bad. I know I done some shit, and been in some trouble, Tami, but I didn't nearly kill that kid."

"I know. Consider it done," I told him.

Just then the guard coughed and we both looked in his direction. His back was turned. I assumed in case we wanted to kiss and maybe feel each other up a bit.

"Thanks for coming," Quincy said. "It was good to see you. You look pretty." I laughed. It was a typical Quincy statement, as though I was a six-year-old going on a picnic.

"Take care," I said and watched as he walked toward the guard. The door closed, and my heart sank.

Out in the parking lot, I cried like I hadn't cried in a while.

Those confining walls. Those sad uniforms were what Quincy had become. No wonder Miss Dee looked so sick. I had only been there about a half hour, but I felt absolutely drained.

❤❤❤

When Tyrone arrived at my house later, he brought Chinese food, and the movie *Casablanca*. I kept staring at him as I lay with my feet in his lap—his hands slowly caressing and massaging my calves and my feet. I liked watching him, when he didn't know that I was watching. I studied the way his forehead crinkled when he was confused about something on the TV. I liked the slow, beautiful way that his mouth turned up into a smile. I liked the playful way that his eyes twinkled and then lit up when he laughed. Sometimes he would look over at me just to check that I had found it funny, too. When he caught me staring at him, I'd quickly laugh as though I had been paying attention to the television.

Later that night, I thought of nothing else except the way he made me feel, and the way that I wanted him to feel. I liked the mixture of passion and aggression. I liked the fact that when I closed my eyes, I wasn't sure if he was in my head, or if I was actually telling him what to do and he was doing it. When I walked in the house that evening I was preoccupied with Quincy's situation. But later, with Tyrone in my bed, I could hardly even remember my damn name.

In the morning I was in no mood to part with him. I convinced him to call in sick. We spent most of the day in bed making love, and talking about dreams and the future. When Tyrone insisted he finally had to leave, it was to have dinner with his grandmother. I couldn't object to that.

Once Ty had left, I called the penitentiary. To my surprise, they gave me the name of Quincy's lawyer and his number without a hassle. His name was Parker Cambridge. On what planet do black people name their children names like that?

The lawyer's secretary transferred me to his line without much of a wait.

"Mr. Cambridge?" I asked.

There was a brief mumble from him. "I'm a close friend of one of your clients. Mr. Quincy Baker. He's in Roosevelt Penitentiary right now. I wondered if I could meet you to have a word with you about his case."

There was a shuffling of papers from his end of the phone.

"Quincy who?" he asked. I fought to keep the steam back. He didn't even remember Quincy's name.

"Quincy Baker. You can glance over your files before I get to your office. I hope you have some free time in the next couple of days. I need to see you as soon as possible."

I knew I sounded commanding, but I didn't want to be jacked with. I felt like this man would mess with me if I let him.

"I…uhhh… guess so. I have this hour free. So if you can get to Broadway in Queens within the hour, we can talk," he replied.

"Perfect!" I exclaimed. "I'll be there."

He gave me the address, and I flew out of bed.

After my shower, I wrapped my hair in a bun and dressed very carefully. I donned my black, pin-striped pants suit and a white long-sleeved shirt which I flipped its collar over the top of the jacket. And then I changed my mind again. I took the jacket off and unbuttoned a few of the top buttons. Nice! I threw on my sunglasses and a pair of stilettos. No one was there to tell me I looked hot, but I knew it. My intention was to intimidate the little shit, as much as I could.

I had fifteen minutes to spare, when I finally knocked on his office door. He had a tiny little office, with two cubicles on a nosebleed floor of the Broadway building. One was his secretary's cubicle, and the other was empty. His secretary notified him that I was there by banging on his door. He threw it open and glared at her. He seemed floored when he finally looked at me. Maybe he had been expecting trailer trash, or a ghetto princess. I stood up to my full five feet ten inches. I strode over to him and grasped his hand in a firm handshake.

"Nice to meet you. I'm Parker." His smile revealed a row of perfectly bleached, white teeth. He had incredibly light skin and deep furrowed brows. Quincy was right about the dreads. They didn't suit him. Parker Cambridge was the type of man that you may give a second glance if he was in a suit. He led the way into his office. I looked for somewhere to sit. The only free chair, however, was covered with papers.

"Please have a seat." He pulled a chair from behind the door and placed it in front of his desk. "I'm sorry. Did you tell me your name?"

"Tamara Jones," I replied.

We both sat down.

"I've got the file on Quincy right here." He opened up a folder.

"You haven't spoken to him," I said flatly.

"Things have been quite busy. I was planning to do that this week."

"Aren't you being paid to make time?" I snapped.

He sighed and looked around the room at the papers in front of him.

"Miss Jones. I appreciate that you care for your...your…Quincy. But perhaps you don't understand how Legal Aid works."

"What is there to understand?" I asked. "He's innocent!"

"Well, I'm not at liberty to discuss the details of his case with you, Ms. Jones," he retorted.

"I can see it in your face that you think he is guilty. You're defending him. You're supposed to believe he's innocent."

"Not necessarily. I'm *supposed* to do what I can."

"You've got an innocent man in prison that you haven't even paid an ounce of attention to. How are you doing your job?"

"Miss Jones. As I said before, I am not at liberty to discuss this case with you. Particularly because he isn't here. However, I will state there is overwhelming evidence against him that points toward guilt on his part."

I cringed, rolling my knuckles into tight fists so that I wouldn't get up and smack this man down. "How do I get him another lawyer?"

"Another lawyer?" He laughed. "That might be costly."

It became clear to me at that point that the color of my skin automatically put me in the "not worth his time" pile. He thought I couldn't afford another lawyer.

I stood up and straightened out my blazer.

I observed that hungry, desperate look of a man that has been starved sexually. He took in the curve of my hips. His eyes slid hungrily up the space between my thighs. There was a noticeable twitch in his eyes as he took in the swell of my breasts, amplified by the extra button I had left undone. I suddenly felt guilty for going to so much trouble to objectify myself. I shouldn't have done that.

"Don't you worry about the cost, Mr. Cambridge."

"I am your best chance. Especially if he will be found guilty anyway. You can save yourself some money," he called as I headed out the door.

I was absolutely fuming. That bastard! Quincy was right. I spun around on angry heels, and marched back to his desk. "For your information, Mr. Cambridge, I probably make more money in a day than you do in a month. I will decide what I can and cannot afford. The extra money they take for my taxes *alone*, probably pays your salary. Quincy isn't going to be found guilty unless you are sitting beside him in a courtroom. If you dislike your job so much, why don't you get a new one? Or, my good man, is an education more than *you* can afford?" I spat. My teeth were clenched as I glowered at him.

He sat in his chair seemingly unfazed. Then I noticed the deep flush creeping into his neck and slowly his cheeks. Here I was making this black man turn red, and was incredibly proud of myself.

"I'm just telling it like it is, Miss Jones. Don't insult me," he said, sounding composed.

"Your presence insults me!" I responded.

He looked embarrassed, and I knew it was because I could read him well. I tossed him one more "don't mess with me look" and stormed out of his office. I winked at his secretary whose mouth was wide open. Then I stormed out of her office, too.

Outside on the sidewalk, I stood gulping in deep breaths as though I might actually run out of air. I knew then that I had a problem. I had just fired Quincy's lawyer and hadn't the slightest idea where to find a new one—or if I even could. I was knee deep in shit.

Ten

I sat on Tyrone's couch. He was softly kneading my feet with his large, warm hands.

"I need a lawyer."

He mumbled a little, as though extremely confused. It was clear that I had caught him off guard. His hands paused, and simply held my feet.

"It…it's for a friend." My voice came out broken. Each word left my mouth sounding foreign and unique.

"Is everything all right?"

"It's all right. It's okay. I mean, it will be. Once I get a lawyer." I sounded unsure of each word that came out of my mouth.

"I know this guy from my fraternity in college. He went on to Harvard Law. He moved back to the city about four years ago. I can call him. He owes me a solid."

"Did you just say a 'solid'?"

He grinned from ear to ear, and then began working his magic on my feet again.

❤❤❤

When I finally met Mr. Donelli he surprised me by being prepared. He had already done some research on Quincy's case.

"We need to request police records. I need to schedule an interview with his old lawyer. Yes, unfortunately I need to meet with him. We have work to do."

"I'm so relieved," I whispered. It wasn't until it was out of my mouth that I realized I had said it. I felt as though an enormous weight had been lifted off my shoulders.

"Good. Let's get Quincy relieved, too, shall we?" he asked, and winked at me with confidence that he could do just that.

Six of us were hiding behind the kitchen door, straining our heads to hear what was transpiring between Precious and her husband. He had dropped her off late at Traci's house. The rest of us were sitting in the living room, and jumped up to hide behind the door when we heard their raised voices and the door slam.

"If you're expecting breakfast in bed, then you best find your ass sleeping in the damn kitchen."

"All I'm saying is it wouldn't hurt you to do something for me every now and then."

"What you think? I like having all your babies running around grabbing at my clothes, and touching my hair and shit. You've lost your mind. I am not having this baby for me. This baby *is* for you. So, don't say I don't do shit for you," Precious yelled.

"I'm going home. What time should I pick you up?"

"I don't know yet."

"Woman, don't think I am waiting up all night for you to call me. This is crazy. You're not yourself."

"I can take her home," Jaclyn whispered to us, as though this solved their problem.

"I don't have brain damage from being pregnant, you know," Precious yelled. I had a feeling that she knew we could all hear. Precious was making a statement. She wanted us to know she was already in a mood, and not to piss her off this evening. "In fact... You know what? Forget that! Go home! I'm done with this conversation!" Precious said loudly. We all jumped up and over each other, as we scrambled to make it back to the couch. We stared absently at Traci's big-screen television where *Waiting to Exhale* was playing. I looked over at Daeshondra who was still craning her head toward the kitchen door. I nudged her hard in the side. She glared at me, and then fought hard to control a laugh.

We heard the back door slam, and then Precious came into the living room. She stared at us all.

"Don't you bitches act like you wasn't just standing with your ears to that door. I know you all too well to give you the benefit of the doubt. I'da done the same shit!" she said. Our resolve crumpled and we exhaled. She failed to elaborate on the reason for their fight, and none of us dared ask.

"Let's get to cooking, because I am hella hungry," I said. Everyone nodded pleased for the distraction.

A Nat King Cole CD blared from the stereo in the kitchen. We were cooking supper and laughing to that breaking point where your stomach feels bloated and pained. Dae sat on the counter. She was supposed to be shelling peas for some dish that Olivia was cooking. But, I swear she'd been holding the same pea pod for twenty minutes. Shan had her extra-large African rear end sticking out of the fridge. Olivia kicked her in the ass as she walked to the stove. Jaclyn was making a salad because her high-maintenance ass cannot cook. I thought I was tall, but Jaclyn is about a half-inch short of six feet. She had her long, dark, firm legs propped on the counter. Precious was there, too, but spent most of the time running to the bathroom to pee. It is true. Pregnant women do spend ninety percent of their day peeing. Traci was cooking some oxtail stew. I cannot articulate how much I was looking forward to it.

❤❤❤

Jaclyn left her salad and stumbled over to the fridge. She was already drunk out of her tree. In fact she had started drinking before most of us even left our houses. She had been sitting on Traci's couch drowning her sorrows, whatever they may be for the week. We suspected her alcoholic ass would be intolerable before the night was up. I love Jaclyn, but not enough to hold her hair while she vomited.

Precious came waddling into the kitchen. She took one look at us and propped her hands in disapproval on her hips. "Would you heifers cook already, dammit. I'm starving."

Before I could stop myself, I had said, "When aren't you starving?"

She glared at me. Then quite loudly said, "Look at this." We all turned around to stare at her. She looked at us as though we should know what she was talking about.

"Fat! I'm fat. I'm so flippin' fat, I can't stand it. I can't even look at myself in the mirror. I'm *that fat*!"

"Yeh...you are kinda fat!" Olivia piped in and the rest of us nodded. Precious looked crushed for a moment, then ran her hands over her belly, and burst out laughing.

"Three hundred bucks for anyone who can get this thing outta me right now. Four hundred bucks. Five hundred bucks."

"Are your feet still swelling?" Liv asked Precious, who shimmied her body onto the stool at the island. She did so with great difficulty. Before some comment about her trials could be voiced, Liv rubbed her hand across Precious' swollen belly.

"Yeah! But that's not from the one in the oven. It's from that bastard I'm married to. He doesn't do a damn thing around the house, you know? I'm on my feet all damn day. I'm chasing kids, making dinner, fixing shit he should be fixing. Then he has the nerve to come home at night wanting to put his feet up. He wants dinner ready and his kids to bring him the damn paper. Then he wants to cuddle and feel me up at night. My boobs have swollen to the size of watermelons. I breathe on them and they hurt. Yet he wants to squeeze them because it turns him on. So you know what I did? Last night I sent the kids out to play. So no one was bringing him his damn paper. I fried some jam sandwiches for his dinner. I gave him a warm beer. Lucky for him he had enough sense to eat his dinner in silence. He pretended he liked it and kept smiling at me. For once, he had enough sense to know that I ain't playin' with his ass," Precious ranted.

"I say," Precious continued, her voice suddenly taking on that dynamic preacher sound. "If he wants breakfast in bed. Tell him to sleep in the damn kitchen."

"We know. We already heard that," Shan piped up.

I laughed so hard my sides hurt. Tears began to pour out of Liv's eyes and she wiped them away while trying to breathe.

We stayed up much too late, eating and talking. It was well after three when I finally rolled into bed, exhausted, but content.

❤❤❤

Quincy had been in jail for almost three months. When Quincy's new lawyer, Marcus, called to tell me the trial date was set for May seventeenth, I cried. I was so frustrated and angry I didn't know what to do. It would be a year since the assault had even taken place. I kept thinking, the kid just got roughed up. He didn't die. The fact that they wouldn't let Quincy out on bail was perturbing, to say the least. The thefts and the break-ins were stupid, but he had never harmed another individual. Marcus explained that under the penal code, no constitutional right to bail exists. The judge— a strict, conservative man—had decided to make an example of Quincy. Although Quincy's prior violations of the law were not related to battery, he *did* have an assault charge from a barroom brawl. The judge felt his prior violations showed he had no regard for the law. And, since there'd been an increase in drug- and gang-related assaults, he had no choice but to remand him without bail.

In the meantime Quincy seemed to have settled into things in jail. That scared me. His mother still went to see him every Sunday. My mother would call me after each visit Miss Dee made to the jail. I soon tired of hearing how brokenhearted Miss Dee felt. She wouldn't be able to handle it if he was found guilty

Quincy was in exceptionally good spirits when he came through the door. He actually kissed me on the cheek as he sat down.

"Hi!" He was hardly able to contain himself.

"What's up?"

"Nothing. Why you lookin' so hot?" He gave me the once-over and I winked flirtatiously. I chomped on my gum a bit.

"Don't I always look hot?"

"You know you do." I blushed immediately. "I have something for you," he said mischievously.

"What?" I asked. "Did ya pick some prison dandelions?"

"Right...*so* I'll just be putting them back in my pocket." He chuckled.

"No really...what?" I was genuinely curious.

"Later!"

"Unh-unh...I can't wait that long."

"Twenty minutes ain't all that long."

"Seems like a lifetime sometimes," I retorted.

He changed the subject. "Did you leave Tristan yet?" He meant Tyrone, of course.

"Why would I leave him?"

"Came to your senses, I guess."

I glared at him. "Maybe it's you that needs to come to your damn senses."

"'Bout what?"

I didn't answer. "So Marcus is interviewing Trey and Shoop, right?"

"Yeh! What you mean by me comin' to my senses?"

"Nothing! How's that computer course you're taking in here?"

"I'm a get my typing certificate." He chuckled to himself. In spite of myself, I laughed at him.

"Did you know that Tycho, the Father of Astronomy, had a pet elk? It died after breaking its leg while going down the stairs, drunk," I said suddenly.

Quincy burst into hearty laughter, so infectious that I couldn't help but laugh, too. The guard looked over at us from his post at the window and smiled. For a moment, I thought to myself, *jails are not that bad*.

"You're weird, you know that?" he asked.

"Don't know where that came from."

"I love it!" He cried, and smiled.

He once told me that I remembered things no one else ever did. He said my mind was a plethora of useless information. He was right.

"Time!" the guard said from the door. Quincy stood up.

"Wait!" he said, and began to fish in the pocket of his shirt. "Here!" He handed me a white envelope. "For when you get home."

"I'm not going home right away. So…I better be able to open it on the way without having to call the cops. I don't want to have to go in for questioning about your escape plan."

"Very funny, Strawlegs." His comment caught me off guard. I hadn't heard that nickname in years. I had totally forgotten it. He used to call me that when we were six. "Where you going? Out with Taron?"

"His name is Tyrone. And no, he's in Canada on a business trip. Jaclyn has a show in New York tonight. It's the Neiman Marcus charity event. It's gonna be hot!"

"All right. I see."

"I'll read it when I get home," I told him with a smile. Then I got up and gave him a light hug and a kiss on the cheek.

When I closed the door of my car I felt as though a weight was lifted off my shoulders. I was in good spirits because Quincy was in good spirits. That made me feel great.

"What's wrong with Jaclyn?" Daeshondra asked me. I shook my head with uncertainty. This was Jaclyn's third walk down the runway. Usually Jaclyn's runway walk was fierce. Her attitude normally made such a strong powerful statement. Yet, here she was walking as if she had no purpose. Each beautiful outfit she had on seemed to disappear on her dejected frame.

"She looks like her damn dog died," Shan said, leaning forward in her seat and whispering to all of us.

Jaclyn paused at the end of the runway, then she stopped short, her hands propped on her hips. She seemed to me like a small child walking in her momma's too-big heels, pretending she was a supermodel. Her usually assaulting eye contact with the audience was lost on the entire crowd. There was no fire behind those eyes. This was a Jaclyn who did not know she was one of the most popular supermodels in North America.

"Get her off the stage," Devora hissed. A woman in front of us turned around. I expected a glare, but she seemed to understand that we knew Jaclyn. Her look was apologetic. It said, *I'm embarrassed for you ladies.*

Later in the reception area we stood waiting for Jaclyn to come out and greet us. We had been nursing our drinks without much enthusiasm. I was certain it was Jaclyn's obvious degenerative state.

The room was filled with important people. There were buyers, sellers, designers, television personalities, celebrities, agents, and models. The seven of us kept breaking conversation as we looked around waiting for Jaclyn. I kept checking my watch. It was after six. The show had finished at five-fifteen.

"You're standing too close to me," Shan said to Traci. Shan gave her the once-over. Traci stood up taller. She looked sexy as hell in a long, slinky black dress that dipped low in the front and in the back. She appeared to have a little more wonder in her bra today, because her boobs were poppin'.

"Drop it like it's hot, girl," Precious said, teasing Traci. Traci turned around playfully and dropped her behind. We cheered her on.

"I really don't like standing this close to her," Shan said, paying no attention to the attention we were giving Traci.

"Why the hell not?"

"Because *hussy*, I know you like to get noticed. That doesn't happen when you're chillin' with me. I can't help it. I'm that good looking," Shan replied.

"When does Tyrone get back?" Devora, asked attempting to change the subject. "Tuesday evening," I responded. "He's been really busy this past week. I've only spoken to him twice."

"What?" This from Daeshondra.

"He's busy," I replied defensively. "I totally understand."

"Whatever! Last month the man was acting like he wanted to run off to some tropical island with you. Now he's too busy to call you when he goes out of town on business?" Daeshondra asked vehemently. "If you ask me, he's out there visiting his *real* woman."

"What do you mean *real* woman. What am I?" I asked defensively.

Olivia shook her head. "Shut up, Daeshondra. What the hell? Why you gotta say shit like that?"

"You shut up. Mind your own business!" Daeshondra chided.

Shan reached forward and gave Olivia a poke in the shoulder.

"There's no need for any of you to talk to anyone like that. Neither of you are minding your own business. Besides, when's the last time you were with a man *for eleven months*, Shaquonda?" Precious asked. "So you can't talk. I think Tamara knows him a little better than you do. She's the one in love with him."

I widened my eyes in surprise. *I am? Am I?*

"She isn't in love with him. She's in love with Quincy," Devora said suddenly. She then excused herself from the group as her cell phone rang.

"What?" Daeshondra, Shan and Precious all asked at the same time. They all turned to stare at me.

"He *is* all you talk about nowadays," Shan agreed.

"That's because he's my friend," I protested. It sounded less confident than I had intended. In fact I sounded downright whiny.

"You never get the same look in your eyes when you talk about Tyrone as you do when you talk about Quincy," Traci told me.

"Well...that's just. Um...well...excuse me...how is this any of your damn business?"

They had to be far from the truth. I mean, I only talked about Quincy because of his current situation. I mean...you talk about people that you see often. Isn't that how it goes or something? Yes! That is exactly how it goes.

"Is that Taye Diggs?" Traci asked. We all followed her gaze. Toward the cocktail bar, he stood talking to a man that was obviously a fashion designer. He had a measuring tape around his neck.

"Hell yeah. I need my groove back," Devora piped up.

"Oh hell no! Someone please remind this heifer that she is a married woman," Shan whispered. With that she handed Devora her glass of wine and left our little circle.

My phone rang and I excused myself as I fished inside my purse for it. I looked puzzled at the name. Jaclyn Thomas.

"Where are you?" I asked as I slipped behind a curtain in the corner of the room.

"I'm in the back. I can't come out. I'm sorry."

"Are you okay? What happened? What's the matter?"

"I'm all right. Really. I just...Thanks for coming. Thank the girls for coming for me."

"Okay. Jaclyn...you want me to come back there and see you?"

"No. I'm good," she whispered, her voice sounding unsure.

"Call me tonight. I wanna talk to you," I said, trying to hide my concern.

"Okay. Hey, again, thanks for coming. Thank them, too."

I hung up feeling confused. I went back to the group to relay Jaclyn's message to them.

It wasn't until I was in my car on the way home that I remembered Quincy's envelope. The moment I remembered it, I had to fight the need to pull over and read it.

At home I put on some music. When Musiq Soulchild was *shoop-shoopin'* on my stereo, I lit some candles. I rummaged through the freezer for a TV dinner. I tossed a Hungryman's fried chicken with mashed potatoes in the microwave. Finally, I sat down to open the envelope. The phone rang and interrupted my mission, however.

"It's me."

"Can I just call you back in…," I began, but was interrupted.

"There's this man."

"Jaclyn. There is *always* a man," I said, feigning exasperation.

"No, but this is different. I actually like him."

"You said that about Damian, and Francisco, and Nigel…wasn't that his name? Then that guy, the broke *and* drunk-ass wine connoisseur from Pennsylvania. What the hell was his name again?"

"Liam."

"Yes…then there was the Russian guy who couldn't speak any English. Ah…and how can we forget Raoul? The Italian guy you met in Florence who was using you to get his green card."

"I get that, Tamara. But, when I tell you this one is different, I mean it is different."

"I've just gotta finish something. Why don't we meet in an hour at Euphoria for drinks?"

"Is Ty there?" she asked.

"No!"

"Because, bitch, I know you better not be blowing me off right now in my time of need. Why can't you meet me now? This girl will be blown off for no man." She stopped and laughed. "Unless I'm being blown by a man."

"It's not a man," I retorted, relieved that she was beginning to sound like the Jaclyn I knew. I flicked Quincy's envelope with my fingers. I wasn't lying; it wasn't a man.

"All right. I'll meet you at Euphoria at ten."

"Sure."

Finally I was able to get back to the envelope. My fingers ripped open the envelope as though they had a mind of their own.

> *I've never truly been in love,*
> *Not the kind they say drops you to your knees*
> *Not the kind they say takes your breath away*
> *Or empties your heart when it leaves*
> *I've never had my heart broken*
> *Never had my world collapse*
> *But last night imagining my life without you*
> *I knew to live each day as my last*

I sat up as I read the last few lines. Questions began to race through my head. He'd written this? Was it for me? My heart felt as though it was beating in my throat. My head had instantly begun to spin. It was good. In fact it was damn good. It was sweet. It made me feel something I couldn't quite explain. How long had he been able to write like that? Move another person like that? For a moment I just sat there clutching the paper. Then I read it over and over again. It was so simple. It forced me to think about the complexities behind each word. And, in turn, I thought about the complexities of the emotions Quincy was feeling to have written this. Finally, I put it in a box in the back of my closet. I keep things like date memorabilia, concert ticket stubs, love letters from old boyfriends. It was my box of nostalgia.

When I arrived at Euphoria, Jaclyn was already there. I noticed a surprising change to her posture and appearance as I sat down. Jaclyn sipped long and hard on her martini. I stared at her shocked. I was unable to comprehend this new Jaclyn. She was generally very much in control of her emotions. In fact, every time she claimed to have fallen hopelessly in love with some other man, there was always a very strong sense of insincerity there. Jaclyn loved money, she loved expensive things, and she loved power. Never in a million years would I ever have thought a man would be responsible for Jaclyn's undoing.

"How'd you get here?" I asked after staring at her as she sipped her drink with a forlorn expression.

"Drove."

"I'll be taking you home tonight. Listen. What is this about? What happened?"

"I think I love him."

"Who is him?" I asked. We were sitting at one of the stools in the hippest new martini bar in New York. Euphoria was known for its delicious martinis, with witty names like Sex Me I'm Hot! and Got the Beach House and the Car. It sported a very modern look with expensive lamps, and lush greenery shown off in cherry-wood flower pots with leather accents.

"David," she muttered. And as if the mere muttering of his name hurt her, a tear spilled down her cheek. She let it fall. I stared at this tear, which in my opinion coming from Jaclyn's eyes over a man, was insane. Her body seemed to fold. I reached over to her, and pushed her legs together. Her skirt had begun to ride up her wide open legs.

"Why is David making you cry? This is the first time I've even heard of him."

"That's the point. I knew what you girls would say. But, you… Tammi…you, I knew I could trust with my secret." She took a deep breath, then lifted her glass and tipped the remainder of her martini, olive and all, into her mouth. Her hair flipped backward and then forward. Her normally well-coiffured do ended up falling haphazardly around her face. I could see the runs of her weave. She didn't move to fix it. So I reached over once again. This time I straightened her hair. Her left hand went up in the air as she beckoned the waitress to bring her another drink.

"I need a double," she told the short dark-haired girl who was wearing entirely too much makeup for my liking.

"Sure. Any idea which one?"

"Get me…get me a Your Loss Loser. Double. Stat! Did I say double?"

The waitress looked at her concerned, but once she saw my glass of Coke she seemed content to bring Jaclyn another drink.

"I don't understand why you are so upset. This is good that you have met someone you seem to love, Jac."

"You don't understand. He's different." She appeared to be summon-ing strength to divulge an important point. "He's a preacher."

I balked, and my eyes popped out of my head. I choked on the Coke I had just held to my lips.

"I cannot be a preacher's wife." Another tear fell down her face. "You know me. I am not a good girl at all. I have slept with more men than I know what to do with. I'm frivolous by nature. I do bad things, Tamara. I'd have to give that up. Oh! God…no more of these martinis. I can't cuss anymore. I'd have to go to church. I'd have to go and find God again. Because, because…even though I pray, baby, you know I only pray when I need something from Him. I pray so that He will speed up traffic on Main Street in rush hour. Girl…the worst part is, I'm praying traffic will move so that I can get to my booty call faster. I'm a model. A preacher cannot marry a model. I'm vain. I'm selfish. How can I make room in my life for God?"

"Jaclyn…there is always room for God. You need to make…"

"Oh Lord…what am I gon' do? You see what I mean? I pray when I need something from Him. You know what else is an issue, best friend?" She paused. Her words began to slur. "David… David and Jaclyn can't kiss, and we can't neck. We cannot do *anything* until we are married. Am I capable of that? Why do I have to love him? Why? Why hast Thou forsaken me?"

"Jaclyn, I think this is a blessing. I think that…"

"Do I even tell him how many men I've slept with?"

"No!"

"He was just there in the grocery store beside me. Tryin' to steal my shit. What kinda man of God tries to steal the last chicken from a woman in a grocery store? Then he had to go and smile them beautiful white teeth at me. You know that look, Tamara. That one that says, I was just gon' smile at you like you were a normal person. But, *but*…now I am really seeing you. And, Tammy… he saw me. He saw me. He is still seeing me. Not only is he seeing me, but he wants me regardless of my flaws. Can you imagine that shit? Lord, forgive me. Inshallah," she muttered.

I shook my head confused. Wasn't that a Muslim expression? But, then she was blessing herself and making the sign of the cross. I realized she was extremely drunk. The waitress placed her martini on the table. Jaclyn stared at it for a moment, then pushed it toward me.

"You drink it."

"I'm driving."

"Yes, you are. And you...you are a good girl. Men want to marry you every day. Preachers want to marry you. Popes want to marry Tamara Jones. And, you could do that. You could that do easily because you don't do like bad things," she whispered. She stared at her drink for another moment, then lifted her glass in the air as if to toast. Then she slugged the double back and let out a loud burp.

"You're gonna come home with me, okay?"

"Do you have anything there might I sin to?"

"No! Jac. Nothing that might cause you to sin at my house."

"Good. Jaclyn has to get right with God. You make sure she does." I picked up my purse and pulled my credit card out. There was a new state-of-the-art system to paying here. There was a digitized screen at the table that allowed you to make your payment options right there. You signed your bill with a magnetized pen right on the screen, and it immediately charged to your credit card. I pulled the receipt out of the top of the machine. I picked up Jaclyn's purse and took my friend home with me.

At home I tried to hold Jaclyn's head while she drank some water. She suddenly seemed to come to her senses and looked me square in the eyes.

"I love you," she whispered.

Absently I shook it off. "I know."

"No, you don't. I love you, Tamara." Her head lulled and the remainder of the water fell down her face. She rolled back onto the bed letting out a rancid burp. I smiled to myself and turned the light on in the guest bathroom—just in case she needed to find the toilet. I felt a strong sense of purpose then. I felt needed by someone and I liked that.

I crawled into bed and set my alarm for three hours ahead. I wanted to check on Jaclyn throughout the night. I'd wake her up and force her to drink some water. I lay in bed for a moment thinking about her and her predicament. It wasn't such a bad one. Maybe in Jaclyn's world. In my world, however, she needed a little God. Perhaps the amount she was getting seemed like a lot to her. But, I was certain this would be the life-changing circumstance Jaclyn needed.

I lay in the dark for a half hour thinking, and wishing for sleep. Then I got up and rummaged in the back of my closet. Finally I found my Bible I had gotten when I was a little girl in Sunday school. I crawled back into bed and read until I fell asleep.

Eleven

I kept watching my mother as she fidgeted with the clothes in the basket. The same T-shirt had now been folded three times. Just as she was about to do it again, I stopped her.

"What's wrong?"

There was a relieved yet troubled sigh that came from her lips. She turned around and sat on the edge of the bed. Her arm rested lightly on the laundry basket. She looked at me for a moment. Then she forced a smile.

"I don't want you to worry. But, there's something I should tell you," she said. I froze. Any sentence that sounded like that, couldn't be good.

"My doctor found another lump in my breast. I would have said something sooner but I wanted to wait for the ultrasound and mammogram. I have an appointment to see the surgeon two weeks from now. Apparently they'd like to remove the entire breast in a month. That's if it is what they think it is." She spoke as though the quicker she said it, the less of it I would be able to comprehend.

"Oh my God!" was all I could manage to say. The words slipped from my lips and I wished I could take them back. She could hear the worry in my voice. It was plain as day. My pulse had quick-

ened, and I suddenly felt nervous. The last time they had oper-
ated, they left her with half of her breast. I had tried to buy her
a padded bra, so you couldn't see it was slightly deformed. But,
she had refused. Now they had to take the entire breast off? "I'm
coming with you when you go to the surgeon. How could they
cut off an entire part of your breast, and there still be cancer
there. They were supposed to get it all, Mom. That's why the
surgery. That's why the chemo and the radiation therapy. Why
do you have to go through this again? I'm coming with you."

"You're gonna be at work."

"I'll be there!"

"Tamara. I'm not worried about it. If I was, I'd ask you to be
there. But, it sounds simple. It's small. They caught it early."

"I'm gonna be there." I paused. "Are you worried? Why are they
taking more? They didn't notice there was more?" I asked softly
and sat beside her on the bed.

I turned to look at her. I mean really look at her. Her hair had
stripes of gray, rather than just speckled bits.

"The breast tissue is the problem! There are cancerous cells in
it. If it's prone to growing cancer cells, they have to remove all the
breast tissue. I think they said they can get almost one hundred
percent of the tissue out, by removing the entire breast. If they
don't, it might keep coming back."

"Are you scared?"

She began to wipe imaginary things off her lap. I didn't expect
her to answer me truthfully. She never would. Mom didn't get
scared. "Scared?" she asked. She burst into laughter. "It will take
more than a boob to knock me off this world. I'm not in the
slightest bit scared. The Lord brought me here again for a reason.
He's going to see me through it."

Even if she were lying, I felt a little better.

I felt sad for me, and I felt sad for her. How could I have moved out? I left her alone in this house. I should never have moved out. I thought of my life without her in it. It would be devoid of any meaning and value. I was nothing without her. In spite of the strength I was putting into not crying, the tears came anyway. I sank to my knees on the floor and then turned to her. I rested my head in her lap. I gripped her thick legs and cried until I thought my eyes might dry up. She ran her hands through my hair like she used to do when I was little.

"Awww baby. It's gonna be fine. God is gonna take care of us. We're gonna be fine," she whispered.

♥♥♥

Ty waved from his car as he pulled up. I was waiting outside on the front steps for him.

"Hi, baby," he called, getting out of his car. "You weren't supposed to see these yet."

He reached into his backseat and produced a large bouquet of red flowers. In his other hand he had a big box. My heart flooded over with happiness. Then in the next instant I felt my eyes begin to fill with tears. I loved him. I wanted to call my mother and tell her. What if I couldn't do that a month from now? What if I didn't get to share all the things that I wanted to share with her? What if she never saw me get married? I pulled myself together and threw my arms around him as he reached me on the steps. My emotions were controlling my every move these days. I held on to the thickness of his body as though he could protect me. I wanted to just open my mouth and tell him everything. I wanted to tell him about Quincy and my mom. But I thought it might be like describing snow to someone who had never seen it.

"Are you still coming to dinner tomorrow?" I asked as we headed into the elevator.

"You bet! What do you think of me bringing my father?" he asked. I coughed. I hadn't met his father yet. In fact, it had never even come up. I knew his mother had died when he was sixteen. I also knew that he and his father were very close. Now I had to try and impress his father. Could I do that?

"Umm…yeah," I stuttered. "I mean, of course."

"What?" he asked softly, noting the change in my voice.

As the elevator moved upward, he pulled me close to his side.

"It's just that it seems like we've been dating forever, and I've never met him before. Does this mean there's a change in our relationship?" I had no idea where that came from. But, there it was. I couldn't take it back. I wasn't even sure I wanted the answer.

"Would you like there to be?"

"Do you?"

"Yes!" His answer came quick and with confidence.

The very pleased corner of my heart went fuzzy on me. I smiled.

"I'm saying I'd love you to meet my father, and for him to meet your mother. It's time. Baby, you know I love you. So, what's holding us back?"

My breath felt as though it was caught in my throat. Sort of like that feeling you get when the wind is knocked out of you. He said he loved me. Had I known this all along? Or was this something entirely new?

"Tamara? Did you hear me?"

"You do?" I whispered breathlessly.

"I do!"

And, then this feeling, this completely overwhelming, naturally occurring feeling, came over me. It was the realization that someone really and truly loved me. He loved me and I didn't know why. But, I was happy. I was happy in that way that you cannot begin to fathom or explain. You just know it is there.

"Of course I want to meet your father," I managed to say. I smiled up at him. He simply laughed.

At my door I stopped and turned to face him. "Are you sure you love me?"

"You're not supposed to make such a big deal out of the first time someone says they love you," he said, chuckling. I smiled.

"I had this dream about you. I wanna tell you all about it. But, it's a little too X-rated for this hallway," I whispered, pulling him inside.

Twelve

"Relax, Tamara. What do you have to worry about? You've met other parents before," my mother said as she reached into the oven to remove the chicken.

"I know, but this is the first time I'm meeting only a father. For some strange reason I feel like there is more pressure. At least before, if one parent didn't love me, I could depend on the other to sway the vote. Mom…this is the first time a parent is meeting my parent. So see…" I paused. "You like Ty. Don't you, Mom?"

"I think he is amazing," she replied. "He's marriage material. Don't screw this up!"

Feeling a little better about the situation, I said, "I think he's great, too."

The buzzer rang. I jumped.

"Okay!" I cried, and looked at Mom. Her smile was reassuring and I was grateful for it. She had a feeling about these things, and I knew everything would be fine.

"I'll buzz them up!" Mom called.

I went into the living room to check on Miss Dee. She sat on the couch staring at a commercial. I didn't think she was really seeing the television. I put my hands on her shoulders and kissed her forehead.

"You all right, baby?" she asked me.

"I'm okay. I'm nervous. They are on their way up now. Do you want me to get you something? Tea? Juice?"

"Oh no! I'm fine. I can't wait to meet the boy you chose over Quincy."

"Quincy didn't want me. He chose another lifestyle," I said, laughing.

She smiled, too, but the look on her face said she really didn't agree with me. She patted me on the arm, anyway.

"I'm starved," she said, and eased herself to her feet. Unsteadily, she straightened herself out. She paused, her hands resting on her hips. Then a hearty dose of laughter left her lips. It reminded me of a livelier version of her. It was the one that I remembered from childhood.

I heard Ty's voice then. "Hello."

I looked toward the door.

The two of them stood side by side. Ty looked good enough to eat. He was so tall and handsome, in a black shirt, and black pants. He was freshly shaven, and had gotten a haircut, too. His father was also stunning. I knew he was closer to Mom's age, but could easily pass for a man in his forties. He stood the same height as Ty. He had probably been taller than Ty in his younger days. He wore an expensive-looking gray suit which complemented his salt-and-pepper hair.

"Hi!" I said, smiling, and forcing my feet to move. I took the bottle of wine Ty was holding and smiled at him. The resemblance between the two of them was uncanny.

"Mr. Livingston, it's a pleasure to meet you," I said, and extended my hand. Then I realized how completely formal I sounded and was about to apologize. He pulled me close and planted a big kiss on my lips. He held me at arm's distance and gave me the once-over.

"If you're not gonna call me Dad, then I suggest you call me Trevor," he said. "You are *so* beautiful. Son, I'm impressed."

Ty and I looked at each other, unsure of what to say.

Before we could respond, Trevor found someone else to focus his attention on. "And who is this lovely young woman?" He was talking about Miss Dee. When I looked over she no longer looked so old and tired. He kissed her hand politely.

"He was a commander in the navy. Don't be fooled by his charm. He has had years of practice at every port they ever pulled into," Ty whispered to me mischievously. "I've heard so many stories of his countless seductions."

"You're jealous," I said, poking fun at him. He winked.

He pulled me close and we embraced for a second. "You look so pretty, baby."

"You look nice, too," I said, blushing.

"My dad loves you. In fact, the minute he saw your building, he was impressed. He says a woman that can pick a home can have his heart. I'm not entirely sure what that means. But you have his heart, if you want it. I'd better keep an eye on you. I don't think he'd be above trying to steal my girl."

Dinner went off without any hiccups. Trevor had us all in stitches at the table. My mom and Miss Dee hung on to his every word. In fact, I think Mom may have even blushed a few times. I hardly spoke. I was so impressed by how well everyone was getting along. Ty would look over at me every few minutes with concern. But, I simply shook it off with a smile and jumped back into the conversation for a moment. While they had blessed the food, I had thanked God for His blessings in my life.

"Thank you, baby," Ty said later as he and I rinsed the dishes. "For what?"

"For this evening. You let me in on this part of your life. I never even knew it existed."

I was puzzled. "Which part?"

"The part that explains why you are so damn amazing. The part that gives me a peek into the reasons that you are so strong-willed. The part that makes me want to love you forever. Baby, the part that shows me who the women in your life were. There's something to be said about a woman who already has people who love her. She knows how to truly love, and be loved."

My heart was racing. Could a more perfect statement have been uttered from anyone's lips? I didn't think so!

"You know my mother said something to me when I was in college. She said, 'If any man ever beats you, he should send you home. She said, I can give you the same treatment here, and you know I love you.'"

"I love this idea," he said suddenly, and wrapped his arms around me. He hugged me from behind so invasively I could feel *every* part of his body pressed against my back.

"What idea?" I asked.

"Of you and me," he whispered. He placed a kiss on my neck.

There was something about the tone in his voice that made me unbelievably content.

He spun me around to face him. He pulled me into a firm embrace, then pecked me on the lips softly. The way he looked into my eyes made me lose all control. The kiss on my throat was next. It was so intense my body responded on its own. A groan escaped my lips as I reached up to pull his head closer to me.

"What are you thinking about?" he asked.

"People," I replied.

"What about people?"

"How complex they are, yet how simple at the same time," I responded. A sweet, soft, musical kiss landed on my lips.

"Any person in particular?"

"Not really."

"Can we go in your room?" he asked in a sexy-meets-horny voice. I kissed him on the base of his Adam's apple, because it drove him crazy. He groaned as if in agony and threw his head back. He hauled me up onto the counter, pressing his face into my neck.

"What? Right now?" I asked startled. "Right here?"

"I love the way your mind works," he replied. "I got me a freaky girl."

"It's your mind that works that way. You just *put* that idea in my head. You really want to...?" I began, but didn't have the chance to finish my sentence, because he was already laughing at me.

"The minute we disappear, the old hens and the rooster will know what we're up to. And I am not down with having my father know that I am having sex. He obviously knows, but I still don't like it." He chuckled. Had I not had that same thought just the other day?

"Are you calling my mother and her best friend 'old hens,' Mr. Livingston?" I asked coyly.

"By your crafty exclusion of my father, then you must be suggesting that *he* is an old rooster."

"You said it!" I kissed him before he could protest. Then I slipped slowly off the counter, so that I had to slide down the length of his body to make it back to the floor. He failed to move. His body told me I had turned him on by that single movement. "You're killing me," he whispered.

I needed to spend the rest of my life with this man. *I have to be in love with him*, I thought to myself. *If I am not in love with him, then I desperately need to have my head examined.*

He slipped his hands down the back of my pants and entwined his finger in my underwear. He looked at me, his gaze challenging me to move.

"I'll get the pot of tea going," I heard my mom say very loudly. I knew it was to warn us she was coming into the kitchen.

Thirteen

There was a sob and a whimper as I picked up the phone. I could barely make out the words, "He's gone!"

"Devora?"

"I came back from a three-day flight to Alaska. His things were gone."

"Bobby left?"

"He took all of his clothes. His jackets. His shoes. His toothbrush. Do you think there is someone else?"

"I don't know," I replied, then instinctively changed my mind. She didn't need to hear that right now. "No. He's probably just trying to figure things out."

"Tamara. He took everything!"

"Where are you? Do you wanna meet me for lunch?"

"I can't. I'm doing the Europe trip this evening. I have a lot of things to do. One of them…one of them was to pick up…his dry cleaning." She sobbed.

I was beginning to feel the results of everyone's pain. My mom, Devora, Jaclyn. Was no one except for me happy these days?

"I just don't know what to do. I didn't think he would ever leave me."

"Do you still love him?"

"I don't know what to call what we had. You know we were friends. But, it was like the moment we got married, we were something else. I don't even know why I said yes. I think...I think maybe I felt sorry for him. I don't know. I didn't want to say no. I mean, he put so much effort into that proposal. God... he was so in love. I didn't want to hurt him, you know."

"I know. Call him. Have you done that yet?"

"No! I'm scared to."

"What are you scared of?"

There was a long, lengthy pause. Then she started to cry again. Then in a barely audible whisper, she said, "I'm afraid he might come back."

I was sitting at my desk sorting through some paperwork when Gabrielle, the intern, came into my office. She was carrying a vase of what looked like blue flowers. Were blue flowers even possible? I gawked at the flowers as she set the vase on my desk.

"What's this?" I asked with amusement in my voice.

"These just came for you. Everyone in the office is dying to know what they are."

"Roses, I suspect." I leaned to smell them. They looked like roses, sort of. They even smelled like roses. I still had no clue. I opened the card, and smiled to myself. For a moment I forgot that Gabrielle was still standing there.

The card read:

I know they're blue, not natural, of course, but a bottle of blue food coloring turned them this vibrant color. Why, you ask. Because you look similar to other women. You sound similar, you dress similar and you act similar, but now I know that you are not like any other woman. Different than any natural woman. You are vibrant and one of a kind, not to be duplicated, nor forgotten. I suspect you know this already.

Last night was great. I need a replay sometime soon. I miss you already, and I can tell you right now that I have only been thinking of one thing since I got to work.

Enclosed are tickets to a show that was (until I pulled a few strings) sold out.

I do hope you'll be able to join me tonight.

Call me at work , please.

Love, Ty xox

When I finished reading the letter, I sighed.

Gabrielle cleared her throat to re-establish her presence.

"Roses," I said, my voice wispy and airy. "You can tell every-one that, too."

"Will do, boss." She left my office, giggling to herself.

I read the card again and again.

The show started at nine. I had a meeting until five. I had to see Quincy sometime that evening as well. I would then have to dash home to shower and change. I couldn't cancel after he had gone through all of this. Besides, I was bubbling over with excite-ment.

When I called Ty, he was on the road.

"Did you know that the *Phantom of the Opera* was my favorite Broadway play? The last time they were in New York, I came down with pneumonia and couldn't see the show," I said.

"Perhaps I have an insider. Perhaps not. You'll never know. I just can't wait to see this show with you," he replied. I recognized excitement in his voice. He was so good at uttering these beautiful romantic statements that I was beginning to get used to them. I would just sit silent for a moment, and let my brain process them. First they would send shivers down my spine. Then a warm ful-filled feeling would flood around my insides.

"Well, I'm honored to be with you," I told him.

"What time shall I pick you up or would you like to drive?"

"You can pick me up at eight."

We said good-bye like two annoying high school lovers. We played at the *you hang up, no you hang up* game.

❤❤❤

The first problem came just as I was on my way to my meeting. It was Parys' school. Was someone picking her up? They had called her father and her grandmother, and there was no answer. I was the last person on the contact list.

I felt horrible for Parys. I remembered vaguely her mother call-ing to tell me she was going to Florida to see her uncle who was ill.

I called my boss and apologized that I wouldn't be at the meet-ing. I drove as fast as humanly but illegally possible. When I arrived Parys was just being taken to the daycare center. She came running toward me when she saw me. There was a bright smile on her face.

"Aunty!" she squealed as I kneeled to kiss her.

As I drove away from the school I called my home machine. Perhaps Angela had called. There were five messages. The last one was Angela.

"Please get Parys. I missed my flight back. I called you at work and left a message. It went straight to your voicemail. I called your cell. It said there was no service. So, this is my last-ditch attempt. If you get

this, please go get my child. I am catching the next flight. I'll be back in the morning. Love, I am so sorry. I hope you didn't have plans. Tell my girl how much I love her. There's more. My uncle's giving me money. Lots of it, Tammy. I can go to school. Parys can go to school. Lots of money. I'm rich! I'll tell you later. Gotta go. Bye! Thanks."

I was stunned. A lot of money? Then I was happy. She could finally go back to school. She could make some money. What a relief that Parys could go to school, too. I was so happy for her.

Oh Lord. Angela wouldn't return until the following morning. Meaning, I had a five-year-old girl to care for, a prison to visit, and two tickets to the opera at eight. I couldn't take a five-year-old to a prison. I would still have issues even if Quincy was her father. I couldn't take her to a jail with me.

"Dammit!" I swore.

I looked in the rearview mirror. Parys' eyes were wide.

"Aunty…," she scolded.

"Sorry," I replied. She seemed content with that. I looked at the clock on my console. I was going to be dreadfully late for everything. I called Ty who picked up on the first ring.

"We have a special little visitor. Angela is in Florida. No one else could pick up Parys."

"So The Phantom will have to wait again? Perhaps we can substitute Barney this evening," he said in high spirits.

"God no! Not this time. Especially when you went through so much trouble to get the tickets. We're going. I'll call my mother," I said.

"Great!"

"But…," I hesitated. "Ty, I'm about five minutes from your place. I have somewhere to be. In fact, I'm going to be late. Can I drop her off?"

"Where you going, Sugar?"

I hesitated. Should I tell him? "Ummm…nowhere!" I replied. I don't know why I lied. There was this window of uncomfortable silence. It was the first time I had blatantly lied to him. I just didn't want to tell him about Quincy. Quincy belongs in another section of my life that I wanted to keep separate. I would tell him someday. I would have to. Just not today. It was such an important day for us. I didn't want to ruin it.

"You're going 'nowhere'?" he asked.

"I can't explain," I said quickly. Then I sighed.

"Bring her by." Something in his voice had changed. He sounded a little standoffish.

Briefly, I wondered if I should apologize. Why should I? What would I say? I still wasn't prepared to tell him where I was going.

"Thanks!"

"I can take her to your mother's before I come pick you up tonight. Is that still all right?" There was a small hint of sarcasm. His earlier enthusiasm was now gone. He had every right to feel this way.

"That would be great. Listen, thank you. I really appreciate it," I said.

"Sure….no problem!" Without saying good-bye, he hung up. I felt like shit!

"Okay, Parys. Aunty's friend is gonna take you to my mom's, okay?"

"Okay," she agreed good-naturedly.

I got out of the car and opened the door for her. She very boldly walked up the driveway to Ty who was coming down his steps. I took her bags from the backseat and brought them up the driveway with me. His black Murano was sitting in the driveway, partially covered in soap. He was wearing a thin white T-shirt and a pair of khaki shorts that were almost entirely drenched. He looked sexy as hell, and staring at the outline of his chiseled chest through his wet shirt was making me a little hot.

Uneasily I kissed him once we were standing together.

"Rough day?" he asked. I nodded my head.

"Thank you for those fabulous flowers. They made all the difference to me today. The tickets, too. You can't know how much they mean to me," I said.

"I'm glad you liked them," he said. "I'm washing my car, Parys. You wanna help?"

She began to jump up and down with excitement.

"Go on in, and change into some play clothes then," I suggested. She grabbed her bag from me and ran up the front stairs to the open door.

"You should probably get going, or you might be late," he said indifferently.

I frowned. "Ty...I..." Then I stopped. I didn't know what to say that might make things better.

He leaned over to me, gave me a quick kiss, minus the usual passion.

Fourteen

"Quincy, you forgot to tell me a little snippet of information. Marcus called me not even five minutes ago. Why didn't you tell me about the videotape?"

Quincy was looking out the window again. He looked nervous. "He told you about that?"

"Of course he told me. Do you know what's on the video?"

"Yeah!"

"You hit the kid three times. *You* did, Q. Then the tape cut off. That's pretty damn incriminating, if you ask me."

"Wasn't me. I know how it looks," he said with no emotion.

"What do you mean, how it looks? That's how it is! You lay three punches. Everyone is going to believe you almost killed him."

"Three friggin' punches isn't gonna kill anyone," he snapped.

"Who made you a doctor? Two to the head, and one to the throat. He had head injuries, and arteries were busted in his neck. That is where you hit him! And, you were high. You said you weren't smoking."

"I didn't do it. I can imagine what it looks like to you. And, about the smoking thing. I knew how you were gonna take it. I just didn't want you to think that I was some druggie. You know?"

"You keep saying you know how it looks. Quincy, you lied to

me. You told me you didn't even hit him. You told the cops the same thing."

"I just told you. I *didn't* hit him! It wasn't me," he insisted. His wrists were clenched into a ball. The *I'm irate* vein in the corner of his left temple throbbed out of control.

"I don't know what to think!"

"Think nothing then! So what are you gonna do? Yes, there was a tape! Frigg the friggin' tape! I'm being framed. I saw the tape. The guy looks like me. But it ain't me. It's dark. The tape is cheaply made. It looks like it's made on a damn cell phone camera," he yelled. The guard looked up and frowned.

"Who would wanna frame you? That doesn't make any sense. Who is trying to set you up?"

"That's what I'm trying to figure out. That's what Marcus is trying to figure out."

"That's bullshit. I don't even know if I can trust you. I went out of my way to get you a damn good lawyer. Now I find out you're playing me. You're playing yourself. You're kidding yourself. How is he going to get a guilty man off? Particularly if there is a videotape of you? Hello? Are you in there? Do you understand what this means? Do you need to spend some time in here and think about beating the shit outta people and how to control your anger?"

"I know you should never have gotten involved."

"Quincy, the kid is eighteen. He's like a hundred pounds. You must look like a horse, stepping on a damn ant. All I asked you for was the truth. You haven't changed at all. I thought you were someone else entirely," I yelled.

"I don't need this. And not from you."

"Who else is gonna tell you things like it is? This isn't for a

B&E; this is for battery and assault. They're going to try to get you for attempted murder. Do you know the time you could do, Quincy? You're a black man beating a skinny white kid. They're gonna chew you up and spit you out in that courtroom. If he dies…you're going to be charged with murder, Quincy. You could be in here till you are a graying, dying, sick ass of an old man. Is that what you want?"

"I know that!"

"Did you do it? Did you almost kill him?" I don't know where it came from. But I had to ask. The tables were turning. There was a tape. Quincy had lied to me, and Marcus was sounding less hopeful on getting him off altogether. Quincy could serve a minimum of two years in that place. I wanted to know the truth.

"Fuck you, Tamara!" he spat vehemently.

"You did *not* just speak to me like that! I'm gonna pray for you and your soul, Quincy. I came here to help you. To be a friend to you. You have the nerve to cuss me?"

"I'm sorry," he said much too quickly. His eyes begged for my forgiveness.

"Quincy, answer the damn question. Just because the tape cut off, does not mean you didn't hit him again. That you didn't deliver the blow. Did you almost kill that kid?"

"I thought you were my friend, at the very least. I don't know you at all." He stood up.

I had only been there for five minutes.

"When were you going to tell me that you hit him? Did you think no one would find out? There were witnesses. Why on Earth would you lie about that?"

"Don't come back!" he said angrily, and nodded to the guard.

When the door closed behind them, I began to cry. He had

lied to me. How could I help him when he lied to me? On top of that, he was guilty. Had he hit the kid until the arteries in his neck burst? Had he hit him until his eyes bulged out of his head, and his jaw snapped? Those were cruel acts. I was afraid. I thought I might even be more frightened because I thought he was still that boy I had loved once a long time ago.

When the door opened to let me out, I was still crying, but I didn't care!

Later that evening I sat on my couch dressed in a long, red Donna Karan evening gown. It was sexy on the rack, and even sexier on me. It had set me back five hundred and eighty-nine dollars, but I had to have it. I was wearing a matching pair of red stilettos and had done a glamorous up-do to my hair. I looked fabulous; I just didn't feel it. And now it was almost twenty after eight. I sat holding my clutch. My legs were crossed as I waited. Ty was never late. I hadn't heard from him all evening. Had I seriously pissed him off, and jeopardized our relationship? Had I done all that to help Quincy? The same Quincy who had lied to me, the one who I could not depend on and could not trust. Why had I done that? It was like I had an inner need to sabotage my own life. If Ty had changed his mind about this evening I was going to fall apart right here on the couch.

Ty hated me, and Quincy hated me. Bad things happen in threes. Who was next? There was a knock on the door. Perhaps it was Lois from down the hall. I dragged my feet, and pulled the door open.

Ty stood in front of me, looking like Adonis. He wore a black tux, with tails, a bow tie, and cufflinks. He was breathtaking. I felt like the wind was knocked out of my sails, as my eyes devoured every inch of his beautiful frame tucked deliciously into his tux. A tear fell down my cheek. I didn't feel it until it was in the middle of its slow descent. It was as if it was carefully calculating the best possible route to ruin my makeup. Before I could reach up to brush it away, his lips found it. He kissed my cheek softly.

"Are you all right, baby?" he asked.

I nodded as confidently as I could, and although I felt like crying for a thousand years, no more tears fell.

"Were you sitting in the dark? Is it because I'm late?"

"No, I just..."

"C'mon, tell me about it in the car." He took my hand and led me to the elevator. In the car he carefully pinned a white corsage on my dress. I smiled as his fingers tenderly found the bottom of the pin, and fastened it. The hand he used to anchor the flower brushed against my chest. The silence made his touch even more intense.

"My father was at your mother's place. So that's what made me so late. Imagine my surprise? They were sitting on the deck with Miss Dee chatting when Parys and I got there."

"Oh. Okay," I whispered.

"You look amazing. I'm the proudest man today. I am the luckiest man today. I want everyone to know how you grace my life. You allow me to be with you. I can't say thank you enough for that," he said happily. It seemed things were back to the way they were. I was so relieved, that suddenly my downtrodden spirits felt lifted.

❤❤❤

Ty spent the night. Around one a.m. the phone rang. It pulled us from each other's embrace. I lay there dazed and confused. When we were somewhat oriented, he picked up the phone beside his head. "Hello?"

There was this look that washed over his face. It was strange, and it was confused. "Yes…one second." He handed me the phone.

"Umm…yes?"

"I can't sleep. I feel horrible!"

"Isn't it too late for them to let you call?"

"You watch too much television, Tamara!" Quincy said reproachfully. "This jail isn't like that."

"Oh!" My heart was pounding.

"I'm still mad. But, I can't sleep because I swore at you. That was really out of line. I'm sorry I disrespected you like that."

"That's okay!" I said.

I felt trapped. Ty turned over on to his side. He was now facing away from me.

"Good night," Quincy said.

"Okay. Good night."

The phone went dead.

I pressed the power button and put the phone on my nightstand. I lay for a while staring at Ty's naked back. I felt guilty. Instead of saying something, I simply shoved my arm under his. I reached my hand up so it rested on his chest. I pressed my body as close to his as I could. At first he felt like a dead weight. Then, after a few minutes, his hand found mine. He entwined our fingers.

Fifteen

Before my mother's surgery, Ty took me to Pagliaci's for our one-year anniversary. But, this man couldn't just pick me up for dinner. He couldn't just purchase a small gift for me and bring it to dinner. No, he started sending me presents twelve days early. Each morning when I walked into my office a rose lay in the middle of my desk. On a piece of paper he wrote one of the many reasons he loved me. I loved how romantic it all was. He was the first man in my life who romanced me without the ultimate goal of getting me into bed.

I started to feel a little anxious about my gift to him. I had ordered a new camera lens for his camera. He is a closet photographer. He often takes long rides out to rural areas to take pictures of landscapes, barns and animals. The lens set me back twelve hundred dollars. Compared to all of the beautiful things I had received, a camera lens seemed terribly unromantic.

Five days before our date, two hundred red roses were delivered to my home. The doorman let the florist in and they spread them throughout every room. I almost fainted when I walked through my door.

Three days before our anniversary, a knock sounded on my door, and a small golden retriever puppy sat outside my open door. A dog bed, a carrying case, toys and food sat in the hall. I had told him a story once about how I had fallen in love with my aunt's dog. He remembered it was a Golden Retriever.

Two days before our date, I was surprised by another knock on my door. It was a personal masseuse who set up shop right in my living room. His hands worked like magic. All of the knots in my shoulders, back, neck and feet melted away.

❤❤❤

I sat in the limo in my peridot-colored dress, high heels, and my rhinestone necklace. I had been sitting on the window sill looking out for his car when I noticed a limo pull up to the front of my building. I sat up, my heart racing. Waiting for the driver to walk up to the building and buzz was excruciating. I couldn't believe he had sent a limo. When the phone finally rang, I jumped for joy and picked it up.

Once in the limo, I had grilled the driver about our final destination. He had laughed, but insisted he couldn't tell me. A few times I caught him looking at me in the mirror. I would look away and smile to myself. I smiled mostly because I knew I had someone amazing, but was still wanted by other men. My mother used to tell me that I had looks that could hook and sink a millionaire. I didn't want to sink anyone. Yet, sitting in that limo, I felt like I could definitely hook a few millionaires.

"Holy shit!" I whispered. We were in the mountains. I lived so close to them, but had never actually been up in them.

Pagliaci's is situated on a peak that overlooks New York. The peak itself is hidden in the Catskill Mountains. The most beautiful part of the scenery is the mixture of green grass and snow you find up there. It was very posh. It was also frequented by celebrities.

When the limo pulled up to Pagliaci's, the driver came out and opened my door. I smiled as he took my hand to help me out of the car. I wondered if I should tip him, then thought, *Ty would definitely have taken care of that already.*

"Enjoy your evening, Madam," he said to me.

Ty stood in the doorway, grinning from ear to ear. As I walked toward him, he slowly and carefully admired my outfit. His eyes finally rested on mine. He bowed gracefully, then kissed me softly on the lips. Even the way he smelled filled me with feelings of romance.

As we sat through dinner, he spoke candidly of his plans for us to go on a trip to Europe. It was the combination of atmosphere, smells, sounds, candlelight and romance that distracted me. I felt as though I was looking at us having dinner. I was overwhelmed with the sheer magnitude of this situation. Here was this man who loved me. In addition to this love, he was a man who could give me whatever my heart desired. Money was no object. Physical boundaries were no problem; he was, after all, discussing a gondola ride in Spain. This was going to be the rest of my life. My heart swelled with pride, with anticipation and hope.

"Baby?"

He pulled me from my romantic side story. "Yes. Sorry."

"Start in Madrid?" he asked. I managed only to nod before I drifted off into my dreamlike state again.

He had the camera I had purchased for him in his hand. After dinner, he opened the door to the patio and we went out into the crisp night air.

"I wonder when they started adding proof-of-purchase seals to all chip bags," I said as we stepped out onto the patio.

"That's a good one," Ty replied, and chuckled to himself. The air up there was amazingly clear. And although we were hundreds of miles above New York, it was still magnificently warm. A sweet, pine, cool breeze took the bottom of my dress and swirled it around my ankles. My hair flew in my face, and when I reached to pull it back, I heard a snap. I turned to laugh at Ty for taking a picture, when he snapped another.

"Do you know how beautiful you are? Extraordinarily so. If it wasn't for your independence, I'd panic each time you left your house. This feels like a dream. You with me. Us, up here, together." I had nothing to say. All I could do was feel. What I felt was complete.

"Listen to you. You sound…I don't know, sentimental." I paused, then smiled at him. "I like it."

"You are making my world turn," he whispered in my ear, and enveloped me in a warm bear hug. We stood on the edge of the patio staring out at the view. There were magnificent, snow-capped mountains behind us, and an amazing view of New York City's lights in front.

The two of us walked down the path, until we found a very private bench that overlooked the city lights. He put his arms around me, and held me close to his side. The night was positively magical. I kept wondering when it would end, because it was honestly every girl's dream date. In the city it is a rare occasion when you can see the sky clearly enough to see all the stars. Most of the time, it turns out to be the blinking lights of an airplane or a police helicopter. Up there, however, everything was clear. I could even make out the stars on Orion's belt.

His nose skimmed the bottom of my earlobe. I snuggled closer into the crook of his arm, and rested my elbow on his hip. "What would you say if I asked you to marry me right now?" he asked.

My breath caught in my throat. I knew that he could feel the sudden tension in my body. But, slowly I eased myself back to my comfort zone. A month ago I may have panicked.

He squeezed my shoulders and placed wet kisses on my cheek. "I've never met anyone as complete as you. Everything about you is so well organized; your thoughts, your house, your life. You are just so complete and I love you."

I sat feeling deliriously happy. He was like heart candy. *God, may I never lose this feeling.*

Sixteen

"I'm starving!" my mother griped. She looked miserable lying on the gurney. She was prepped for her surgery and busy getting on the nurses' nerves. I couldn't quite understand how she managed to be in such high spirits. My nerves were shot. One moment I was sitting tapping my feet. The next moment I was pacing around the room chewing my nails. I'd paid too much for my damn manicures to be chewing them.

"Why don't you get some coffee from the cafeteria?" Olivia said to me. I looked over at her sitting by the door. I looked at her as though she had just arrived. But, actually she had been there all morning with us.

"Coffee?" I asked absently.

"Yes…in the cafeteria," Olivia said with a look of encouragement on her face.

"Bring me something to eat while you're there," Mom piped up rather loudly.

The nurse who was hooking her up to an IV shook her head at me. It was a clear no. My mother kissed her teeth angrily.

"These people think I'm playing," she announced. I glared at her.

"I'm not leaving," I told them both. "I'm not leaving."

"Tamara. Stop digging my grave."

"I...I'm not," I protested. The look on her face shut me up, though. I didn't even like the sound of the word "grave." I was just worried, that's all. I turned away fighting the tears. I shuffled over to the window and stared down at the parking lot. The tears would come to the surface and burn and burn. I kept trying to push back the ache in my heart. But, it was bottled with fear and a whole lot of other shit I could not deal with. I really needed Ty right then. But, I couldn't just call him. What would I say? "By the way, my mother has been sick for a while now. I didn't tell you. But, can you come, please?"

Days later when my mother lay in bed recovering from her surgery, I managed to slip from her bedroom to make a phone call to Traci. She showed up an hour later with her hair knotted on top of her head. She wore a paint-stained pair of overalls. I smelled the particularly potent smell that paint has. I looked at her beseechingly.

"I know I smell. I have a change of clothes in the car," she replied and smiled at me, anyway.

"It's just for an hour or two. I haven't left the house. She's just been sleeping so much I don't want to leave her in case she needs something."

"Don't mention it. This is what sisters are for."

The day after her surgery every one of my girlfriends had come by to visit. Mom was generally quite doped up on pain medication and barely realized or recognized them. I had sat vigil day and night. There were so many emotions coursing through my body. I knew she had come out of the surgery okay. Her doctor was pleased it was successful. Yet, there was this tiny niggling feeling inside me. What if they hadn't gotten it all? What if chemotherapy and radiation were ineffective? There could be more surgeries. There could be more pain and more heartache. This might not be finished just yet. As my mind raced, and my mother slept on I became more and more distraught. It was as a result of her constant glare that had kept me from thinking the worst thoughts. Now, she was recovering and no one was here to reassure me anymore. I was doing a terrible job of feeling positive.

I drove home without much attention paid to the roads. I showered, changed into a fresh set of clothes, and then grabbed my briefcase so I could do some work at the hospital. It wasn't until I was driving back to the hospital that I stopped the car and pulled over.

I had to go and tell him. There were no two ways about it. He would make me feel better. Tell me everything was okay. He knew me well enough that the words already would be on the tip of his tongue. I wished I had told him. I turned the car around and headed in the opposite direction.

Seventeen

He stared at me with shock on his face. There was hurt in his eyes. He wasn't hurt that I hadn't told him earlier. He was hurt that my mother was going through it at all. The minute the words left my mouth, Quincy stood up and walked over to me.

"When they wheeled her into her operating room, there was this feeling. It just washed over me. It reminded me of how truly insignificant we are in this world. We cannot control what happens to us. Who knows when your last breath will be, or your last doctor's visit where you are healthy. We have no control," I mumbled.

"You control how you choose to live each day, Tamara. You control the things you can. And, God knows I have sinned so often I have no right to mention His name. But, you pray that He will give you the strength to accept those things you cannot control. I need to learn to follow my own advice."

He pulled me to my feet and hugged away my fears. He hugged away my devastation. He even hugged me until all the tears were gone. The right words poured from his mouth and reached my ears with such certainty I believed she would be fine. It was like he was reaching inside me and pulling out all the things I knew were already there—the answers I needed to feel hope again.

Eighteen

"Has your…okay… let me restart that. Okay, hypothetically speaking, have you ever gotten the feeling that your gyno is flirting with you?" Shan asked.

"Isn't that against the law or something?" Daeshondra asked. "And if it isn't, at the very least it is disturbing."

We were bowling at Aphrodite Lanes on the East Side. So far, only Daeshondra and Shan were present. So, we had claimed our two lanes and were drinking cocktails until the others arrived.

"Hypothetically speaking. I just mean, you know me. I am not about to jump into bed with any man. Is it odd if I were to go on a date with him and he's already seen my coochie?"

I shook my head confused. The sheer magnitude of that possibility was overwhelming.

"Girl, he hasn't just seen your coochie. He's been all up in it six ways since Sunday, honey. He will know that coochie better than you even know it, *okay*?" Daeshondra said.

I had to laugh at that. The remnants of a smile quickly disappeared from my face as Shan's eyes bore angrily into mine.

"Don't encourage her. I'm just saying, I like him. We get along really great. He's so nice…"

Daeshondra cut her off, "He's rich."

Shan ignored it. "He's so kind. He's sweet. He called my office and personally thanked me for the Christmas card I sent last year…"

"He's rich," Daeshondra proclaimed.

Shaquonda finally snapped, "Look here, bitch, you are a virgin. You have a five-month kissing rule. You still live at home with your parents and *you* think *you* have the right to judge anyone?"

"Ladies…ladies…please," I interjected simply for the fact that the people in the lane next to us were passing concerned glances between themselves. "That's not what Dae's doing. She clearly is concerned with the professionalism of this man. Am I right?" Daeshondra nodded. "Really, that's all. No judging here."

Then from behind us, "Who's not judging? Isn't that what we all do?"

We turned around to see Precious standing and putting her shoes on. She rubbed her belly as she prepared to bend down.

"Hope you guys don't mind. We've got company," she said, and motioned with her head to two aisles down where her four children were already putting their names into their screen.

"Let me go see my babies," Daeshondra announced with sudden excitement. She jumped up and went to see the kids.

"I squinted my eyes to get a clearer look at them. There was eleven-year-old Kira, who looked just like Precious, only with lighter skin. There were ten-year-old twins Jerome and Lisa, who looked absolutely nothing alike. In fact, Lisa was a good foot taller, with longer limbs than her pudgy twin brother. Last was the baby, Davey, who was turning five and was definitely sick and tired of being told what to do by everyone. It was Davey who caught my attention.

"Is he wearing underwear on the outside of his clothes?" I asked.

"Yes…it's this phase he is going through. I can't get him to take them off. All this child does is fight and scream. He is so determined to make a statement. I think this is the only thing he can control. I even tried to trick him with the old kindergarten speech. He's so excited about going, I thought that might help. But, this child is as thickheaded as his father. When he sets his mind to be a pain in the ass, he does it so well he puts hemorrhoids to shame."

I smiled to myself.

"How's Mom?" she asked.

"Doing really well. We went to the first appointment already. Everything looks good. Her doctor is so hopeful. He said she will probably not be on the chemo for very long," I told them pleased with the news myself.

"Praise the Lord!" Precious whispered. She stopped suddenly and stared at Shan, who was not rubbing Precious' belly, or at the very least touching it. She was poking and pressing with gusto.

"What's the matter with you? I can feel, you know."

"I know. I just wanna see if it's kicking."

"If you don't stop touching me, something's gonna kick you."

Jaclyn and Devora did not show up. The two of them seemed to be MIA to many of our gatherings. It had begun to worry me. I came to the conclusion that for the sake of the group I would need to interfere in their lives a little.

"Christmas is coming," he said softly.

I knew what he was feeling, because I had felt it, too. Dread, anger, and pain. He would be spending his Christmas behind bars, without his mother.

"She'll spend Christmas with us," I said, and reached across the table for his hands.

He grasped my hands in his and turned them over. "I'm scared," he muttered quickly as though he might change his mind. "I don't wanna be here for the rest of my life. I won't make it!"

"You won't be! Marcus is working hard. Something about the tape. Quincy...you know I'm here for you. Like you were here for me. I'm not going to let them keep you in here."

He looked at me as though he was really seeing me for the first time.

"Time!" the guard called.

Quincy and I stood up and hugged each other.

"No! It's different, you know. The way that you are here for me and the way that I'm here for you," he said. "It's different!" He walked out the door.

Seventeen

On December sixteenth, I stood at my window looking out at the street below. There had been a light snowfall the night before. It had covered everything outside with a soft, beautiful blanket. I loved the first snowfall. It always reminded me of my childhood. Quincy and I would always run outside and attempt to build the first snowman of the year. Our efforts were normally in vain.

It was my first Saturday in months where I could simply sit at home in the morning and slow my life down for a moment. The door buzzer rang and I looked with surprise down at the street. I hadn't even seen anyone approaching. I pressed the intercom button.

"It's Shan."

"Okay," I responded, pressing the button.

When she came through the door she looked frantic.

"Big problem! Huge friggin' problem!" she wailed.

"Sit…talk. Use your words, Shaquonda."

She sat on the couch, hyperventilating a little. She reached into her purse and pulled out a box.

"Is that a pregnancy test?" I almost yelled.

She yelled loud enough for us both, "I know!"

"The gynecologist. Did you sleep with him?"

"I didn't even suggest we exchange numbers," she yelled. "I don't know how this happened. I haven't been with a man in months. Months, Tamara. I have no friggin' idea how, or...what...you dunno. I'm going crazy."

"Well...how late? Months...perhaps it was months ago that you conceived," I suggested.

She jumped up pacing the room and shaking her head. "I'm a month late. I would know. I'm as regular as an automatic bill payment," she cried.

"Okay, we don't know anything yet. Let's do the test. We'll discuss then."

She grabbed the box and began to walk to the bathroom. Before she could get there, however, the phone rang. I hesitated. This might not be the right time to pick up, I thought. I did so anyway.

"Hospital...Precious...baby."

"Jaclyn, is that you?" I asked.

"Meet us there. I can't find Shaquonda and Devora. Call them, please. She's at Our Lady Of Mercy." The phone went dead.

"Change of plans. But, bring the box. Precious is in labor, or going into labor. Already had the baby? I don't know," I said to Shan. She nodded and turned back to me.

"It's gonna be fine! Deep breaths," I whispered. I looked down at my clothes. They were "laze around the house" clothes. I didn't care. I went out anyway.

❤❤❤

Four hours later we were all sitting in Precious' room. We had managed to track everyone down and were now vigilantly watching over her. Her contractions were steady, but it seemed that this baby had no intention of leaving the warmth of the womb. It must be a boy. Every twelve minutes or so a contraction would seize Precious. On one side of the bed her nurse would hold her hand, breathe with her and either swab her with a cool cloth, or rub her belly. On the other side Daeshondra, Jaclyn and Devora stood watch over her. Every time she began to scream their faces would tense as though they were feeling her pain. When it was over they would all begin to breathe normally again and fuss over her. It was Olivia, who already has a child, Traci, Shan and I who were not hovering right over her.

The last contraction ended and Precious looked over at me—her face sweaty, her eyes looking tired.

"Can you try him again?" she whispered breathlessly. "Please. I know. I just…need him here. Not to mention, when this baby comes, their gonna kick all but one, maybe a few of you outta here. I don't want to have to choose. Not today. Find my husband. Please!"

"I'm not even supposed to have a phone on in here," I said as the nurse stepped out of the room.

"Please."

I nodded solemnly. Precious usually acted as though she hated her husband, Curtis. But, here she had seemingly determined to keep her baby inside until he made it there. I guess even dysfunctional love can find a place in this world. I picked up my phone and dialed his cell number. There was no answer. I tried the house line and left a fourth message on the machine. Then I tried his work number again. They said he was still on a job and when he is laying cable lines, he is sometimes in places where his cell phone can not get reception. I hung up and shook my head at Precious. She looked disappointed and forced a weak smile.

Shan sat on the chair feigning interest in the events going on in the room. Yet, she twirled the pregnancy test over and over in her hand.

"I bet you have at least nine minutes till the next contraction. Go in the bathroom and do it now," Traci suggested. At this Shan's face lit up.

"Yes. Why didn't I think of that?" She stood and walked to the washroom. "Come with me."

Traci looked at me as though she couldn't be serious.

"She's not talking to me. It was your suggestion," I responded.

Shan stopped. "I'm talking to both of you. Bring that camera, Tamara."

I looked puzzled. She didn't mean… No…she couldn't mean… But she did mean it.

"I want proof of this," Shan said as she pulled down her pants.

"I can't believe I'm doing this," I whispered. Then the door opened and Olivia came in. She watched as Shan pulled her underwear down and squatted over the toilet.

"You can't do it like that," Olivia scolded. "You're supposed to put the stick in a steady stream of urine."

"It says you can pee on the stick, too. It just has to stay for five seconds. Trust me…my pee is steady. Trust me, too, that it smells kinda funky sometimes. So you may need to hold your nose." She then beckoned me closer.

"I want you to get right close. Take like three pictures."

The simple fact that three of us were crowded into the bathroom while Shan took a pee was disturbing. But, in addition, she wanted me close to catch the picture? Hell no. I would not be attacked by pee splatter. Particularly if it was not my own pee.

All of the noise in the bathroom stopped as she began to pee. I stood right where I was and zoomed in to catch the stream and the stick. When she was all done, we stood dumbfounded.

"Three minutes," Traci whispered, looking at the box. Those three minutes seemed like the longest minutes of our lives. We simply stood around staring at the stick in the sink. And when the plus sign appeared in the "pregnant" window, I lifted the camera and took a picture. We turned to Shan who looked as though she was going to pass out.

Outside the bathroom Precious went into a rather painful contraction because her voice reached ear-splitting decibels. I felt stuck between two evils. Shan looked like death, and Precious sounded like death. Then through Precious' screams, I heard my phone ringing in the room and went out to get it.

"I'm on my way," a male voice said. I could only assume that it was Curtis. I managed to utter the room number before he hung up.

"He's on his way," I told Precious who probably could not hear me.

Out of the bathroom came the girls. Shan sat down in the chair for a moment looking like a ghost. Then she came to stand beside me.

"I'm gonna get it together. I'm going out in the hall. I'm gonna compose myself and be here for my girl. This is her time." Shan walked out the door.

"It was positive?" Jaclyn asked, looking shocked. "Positive? How is that possible?"

"Glory be to God," Daeshondra whispered, squeezing Precious' hand. "An immaculate conception!"

❤❤❤

At one-fifteen a.m., with Curtis by her side, and her girlfriends in the hall, Precious gave birth to a beautiful baby girl. She named her Athena Grace Rollins. She was tiny, weighing only four pounds seven ounces. She looked just like her mother, except with tiny doll-like features. She had gorgeous eyelashes. But, it was the eyes that were a beauty. They were big, brown and much too expressive for a baby. She was stunning.

I looked over at Shan as the nurse pushed the cart holding baby Rollins up to the window for us to see. A tear fell silently down Shan's face.

Twenty

We had our Christmas dinner party at Devora's. With Bobby gone, her large house looked bare and lonely. The flower pot of poinsettias that sat on the kitchen table looked like a desperate attempt to bring joy to the house. Devora wore a thick red sweater and a tight green skirt. But even the festive outfit could not compensate for the sadness on her face.

"You look like crap," Traci said the minute Devora opened the door for us.

"Thanks. I hadn't noticed."

"What the hell is going on with you?" Traci asked, taking her shoes off and placing them in the foyer.

I cast a surprised look at Devora who shook her head. She hadn't told her?

"Where's Ty?" Devora asked me.

"In a meeting. He'll come when it's done."

"I'm desperate to meet Jaclyn's preacher," Traci called from the kitchen. "Girl, what you cooking? Shouldn't this turkey have some meat on it? It looks a little anorexic."

"You didn't tell any of them?" I whispered to Devora.

"No! I didn't know if he was coming back. I mean…I know now. He's not coming back."

"What do you mean you know *now*?"

She looked at me for a moment, then pulled me into the office down the hall. She dug into one of the desk drawers and pulled out an envelope.

"I sure as hell hope this is a Christmas card," I said.

It was divorce papers. I looked at Devora solemnly who immediately burst into tears.

"I'm so sorry."

"He doesn't love me. This is my fault. I mean…I didn't even want him back. But, every time I walk around this house I miss him. There are two sinks in the master bath. He isn't going to spit in there anymore. It's over!" she whispered. I threw my arms around her neck. She sobbed bitterly.

"What happened?" Traci stood in the doorway. Before anyone could answer she threw her arms around us both.

"Bobby left me," Devora muttered through her tears. With the utterance of those words, however, she erupted into a fresh round of tears.

"Is he mad? He left you? Fabulous you!?" Traci said, shaking her head. "What's his number? Let me call him and knock his ass out!"

"It's no use. He's even changed his number. I tried to call his parents in Philadelphia, but they said they didn't know where he was. His sister in Ohio hung up on me. I just…"

There were more tears. When the bell rang, I left Traci to straighten her out. Precious stood at the door smiling at me. She thrust a bottle of wine into my hands and kissed me. I left the door open, because Olivia was parking her car in the driveway.

Precious took off her coat. I looked at her with surprise.

"How the hell do you look so good? Didn't you just pop out a child?"

"What can I say? I am blessed!" She chuckled. "Blessed, and tired as hell!"

"Where the party at?" Olivia said as she came in the door. She pulled off her jacket revealing a sexy, tight, curve-enhancing black dress. Precious and I both turned and gave her a dirty look.

"Where you goin' lookin' like that?" Precious almost yelled. "You forget every man here tonight will be taken?"

"I have no shame. I'm out to find me a good one, *okay*."

"Trifling," I said loudly and took the pot of casserole she had in her hands.

At dinner I could not stop staring at Jaclyn's Preacher Man, David. He was gorgeous. In fact, I stared so much that Ty shoved me under the table. When I looked reproachfully at him he shook his head at me.

"You're staring at him," he whispered. I looked away embarrassed. I tried in vain to avert my eyes, but he was stunning. Before we started eating, he blessed the table. Everything about his voice, his presence, even his hair was distracting.

Conversation floated easily around the room. Devora had prepared a beautiful table of ham, turkey, beef, stuffing, collard greens, mashed potatoes, fried rice, cranberry sauce, green beans, and the most delicious egg rolls. I helped myself to two plates before the argument happened. It stopped me in my tracks, and turned my stomach over.

Olivia was explaining that she had once hit a car. She was reversing, when her phone rang. Instinctively she had reached for it, and as a result of the distraction had backed into the side mirror of a car. She then divulged that she had driven out of the parking lot as fast she could without leaving a note.

"You didn't!" Traci whispered, chuckling to herself.

Precious interrupted, "You know, sometimes you just panic. I did that once. I mean, I ended up going back. But, my first move was to get as far away as possible."

"That's not right. If no one else saw it, at the very least God saw it," Jaclyn piped in. Silence suddenly fell over the table. David's beautiful eyes flitted around the table, but he continued to eat.

"Jaclyn," Daehsondra said vehemently. "*You* cannot talk about God with all those sins you commit. You the most…*loose*…woman I know."

"Excuse me. Who put you in charge? She has found God. She has repented for her sins. She's not being rude. You're being a bitch!" Devora spat. "You are almost thirty years old and still living with your parents. You can't judge anyone, Daeshondra."

It was obvious that Shan could not keep quiet. She was so mad, she stood up and said, "So, you're better than her? You are sitting there all high and mighty, while trying to pretend that the good man that you had is coming home? What is this party? An attempt at bringing Christmas into your home? You ain't got no family; you don't even have a man anymore. So, you have no right to say shit."

"Girls…," I whispered. But, I was met with steely glares. I looked at David and Ty, trying to apologize for this obvious display of chaos.

"You! You have had four men who left you before you even got to the altar. And now you are sitting here talking about even having a husband. Aren't you the same one who is currently pregnant with the gynecologist's baby? You have no idea how this baby got there? Was it the drugs? Which one was it you're taking, ecstasy?" Devora yelled.

Shan's face paled. She wiped her mouth with her napkin, and looked down in her lap. I knew she was composing herself.

"Ladies…please," David said much too softly. Jaclyn put her hand on his arm to silence him.

"Why would you say that?" Jaclyn asked Devora. "Why would you do that? She's not on ecstasy. Regardless…that was low."

"She had no right to call her out like that. Whose business is it if Bobby left her? Not ours if she doesn't want to tell us," Precious piped up. She stood up and walked over to Devora. It was then that I became scared. They were starting to take sides.

"Ask her what those little pills that she keeps popping are. I dare you. Our successful Shaquonda Brown takes ex," Devora yelled. "Don't you ever come to my home and insult me like that. I will leak out all your damn dirty secrets. Every last one of them. I may no longer have a man, but I'm not taking drugs or getting pregnant by random men." Shan was up on her feet. Tears were already running down her face. She pushed her chair back, turned around and walked right out the door. Olivia went after her.

I shook my head at Devora. "Why? Why would you divulge that? Now? Like that?" I asked amazed.

"She can't call people out, especially in their own home. Someone had to put that bitch in her place." Devora's voice broke, however, and she spun around and walked directly up the stairs. Precious followed her.

"I'm leaving. Are you coming?" Jaclyn said to David. He stood up uncomfortably. It was obvious he didn't want to leave. He dropped the turkey leg he was holding.

When they left there was only Daeshondra, Traci, Ty and me at the table.

"Why'd you have to bring that up?" Traci asked Dae. She shook her head seemingly unconcerned.

"At first it was minor. But, your comment blew things way up. It's Christmas, why is this necessary?" I asked her. "Especially because you know that Jaclyn is sensitive about this David situation. What kind of impression have we made now?"

"Is she really taking ecstasy?" Traci whispered. The three of us looked at each other ignoring Ty.

"I don't know. I've seen those pills. I was looking in her purse for gum. They were in a Ziploc baggie. Maybe five of them were in there. When I asked her what they were, she just laughed. She didn't say anything, But I know ex when I see it." Dae whispered.

I didn't say anything. I was pretty certain they were ecstasy. She had told me once long ago that she used to go to raves and took a lot of pills. She said every now and then she just needed a hit. I had never told anyone, but had made her promise me she wouldn't do it anymore.

"The gynecologist got her pregnant and she doesn't remember it? I was thinking all of this time about the fat lawsuit we were gonna have to support her through if he impregnated her without her knowing," Traci said, shaking her head. "I can't deal with all this right now. I'm gonna go home and call Michael. I need to feel grounded right now. This is all too overwhelming."

When Traci had her jacket on she leaned back into the dining room and waved. Even that looked as though it took too much energy for her.

"This is the craziest Christmas dinner I've ever been to," Ty said to me. I simply nodded.

Twenty One

On Christmas Eve, Miss Dee and I took a garbage bag of prison-friendly gifts to Quincy. I was pleased because Miss Dee seemed healthier than she had in months. When we were leaving, Quincy hugged me extra long, resting his chin on my head.

"Are you gonna be all right? Why don't you call my mother's place tomorrow?" I whispered, not wanting Miss Dee or Devora to hear us.

"Why does it say fifty-six varieties on Heinz labels? I only know of one variety, tomato ketchup," he replied.

I pulled back momentarily and then smiled.

Now who had the dumb-ass questions? "Here!" he said and shoved an envelope into my hands.

When I got home I read the papers in the envelope.

"Best Friends"

There are so few we find as we walk,
Ones that we can share with, laugh and talk.
When we find the one that is there,
Life becomes easier as you know they do care.

I have a friend, the one that is meant for me,
She takes the sad away and brings me glee.
I know now I must have done something right,
Today my spirits soar, and as high as a kite!
Mine has opened so, oh so many feelings,
A lot of my life trouble, she is healing.
This friend, my best friend is who I speak,
Her companionship, her thoughts are what I seek.
We know now, we will be best friends forever,
We will cry, we will laugh, we will do it together.
She's my best friend, her name is Tam,
She helps me remember forever, who I am.

Tamara, I know that these poems will not be anything compared to the other gifts that you will receive for Christmas. But, when I think of you I feel inspired. I feel inspired to write silly things, serious things, funny things, just things. And so, this thing, is all I have to give you. Merry Christmas.

"Sometimes"

Sometimes I can see her
In my dreams at night, she
Calls out to me like
She is lost,
forever
Is how long it seems
I have loved her, but
Add a day and you will
Know how much I've missed her

Sometimes I can
Feel her, right here beside me, in
This place she does not belong, nor
Do I.
But how can I tell her, that
Sometimes I can see her and
Feel her and
Want her.
But why should I
When it's only
Sometimes?

I read the poems as though they were a little secret just between the two of us. I also cried. I was a total wreck. His poems were choppy, and followed little or no rules of conventional poetry. Yet, here they had moved me. Here he was sharing his thoughts and I understood.

I was sad for Quincy; I was sad for his mother. I was scared of almost losing my mother. I was scared for losing anyone that had ever been in my life. I was plain sad.

Suddenly I remembered what he had said. What the hell? There are fifty-seven varieties of Heinz, not fifty-six. Furthermore, it's not the different kinds of ketchup, either. It's different food items.

"There are different types of ketchup. Regular, hot, and low-sodium," I said to myself, and then laughed.

Ty came over later that evening. We ate chicken curry noodles, drank red wine, and watched *It's a Wonderful Life*. We made out on the couch like teenagers with clothes on; dry humping. Then we migrated to the bedroom for the real thing like adults.

In the morning I was woken up by breakfast in bed.

"I didn't even know I had actual food in my house."

"You didn't. I brought it last night," he replied. Taking the fork off my plate he put some egg into my mouth. I pulled my knees up to my chest as if to keep all the good feelings inside me.

"I have an early gift for you," he announced. He produced a small box wrapped in red foil paper, with a tiny silver bow on it. I smiled contentedly. I guessed it was a ring. In fact I guessed it was an engagement ring.

"What is this?" I whispered. I tore open the wrapper. There it was. A beautiful, breathtaking diamond ring. There was a tight squeeze in my chest, and I realized I had been holding my breath. I let it out slowly marveling at the sparkle, the clarity, and the sheer size of this diamond. It was a princess-cut, white-gold, single-setting ring. I knew a thing or two about diamonds. Ever since I could remember I'd been checking out wedding rings on my own. This had to have set him back at least fifteen thousand dollars.

"Tamara, I love you with all my heart. Will you spend the rest of your life with me and make me the happiest man on Earth?"

He was kneeling down beside the bed. I almost knocked the breakfast tray over as I leaped off the bed at him. We fell together on the floor.

"I can't believe you did this. Oh my God. It is…it's beautiful. It is the most beautiful thing I have ever seen. I can't believe it."

"Is that a yes?"

"It's better! It's a hell yes!" I screamed.

The week before New Year's Mom had started to look better. She was moving around the house on her own. It was slow and painstaking, but nonetheless mobility. When I opened her front door New Year's Day, the smell of baking immediately assaulted my nose. It was pleasant and comforting for so many reasons, I simply stood in the doorway grinning from ear to ear.

"Child, what are you doing? Don't you know it's winter out there?"

"Hi, Mom." I closed the door behind me as she took a fresh batch of muffins out of the oven.

"I've been up since seven. I was looking at wedding magazines this morning. I've found this absolutely gorgeous invitation you must see. Are you hiring a wedding planner, or do we get to pretend?"

"Umm...I haven't really gotten that far yet. I guess it doesn't matter. If you want to plan it. Or, we can hire someone," I began and then stopped. She had a look of pure contented joy on her face.

There was so much excitement in her voice. I could hardly contain my relief.

"Oh, I'm so happy. I'm so happy. You are feeling better. We are planning a wedding. I love this man. You have no idea," I cried. I threw my arms around her. She squirmed for a moment, then settled into my hug.

Finally, she whispered, "You're all I've got."

A few hours later she went upstairs to lie down for a while. I sat on the bed as she pulled her oldest and most comfortable nightie out of the drawer. It buttoned up the front, and she bent slowly struggling with the buttons at the bottom. I got off the bed, and started to button them for her. When I reached her waist I stopped. I looked at the dark scar that spread across the space where her breast used to be. She looked mutilated, changed and unfamiliar to me. I didn't want her to see my fear so I continued to button. She placed her hands on mine and stopped me.

"This is a part of me now. This scar is part of your mother. It is a part of my identity." Even as she spoke tears came to my eyes. I didn't want her to look deformed to me. I wanted her to look beautiful as she always had. But wasn't she? She took my shaky hands. She ran the fingers on my right hand across her scar. The thickness felt hard like a knotted rope to me.

"It's okay," she told me. "It's okay. It has only made me stronger. These old breasts served their purpose. They fed you and comforted you when you needed it. You're not my baby anymore. But, I've got some sweet memories."

I smiled through my tears.

Ty and I were talking about house shopping, church locations, the dinner menu for the reception, a guest list, a date, even whether we should throw confetti or release doves at the church. I was so overwhelmed with wedding plans, and well, life plans. Every now and then I would realize that I had forgotten to do something important. I'd forget to put deodorant on, or reach the door and realize I was still wearing my shower cap.

In addition to the plans, I was spending a lot more time with Ty. For the past six years, the girls and I had always spent New Year's Eve together. In fact, we had even gone to Cuba together one New Year's Eve. Yet, here we all were, divided and hurt. If they were speaking to me, they were guarded, concerned I might tell the other person about some vital piece of information. Shan, who worried me the most, had not returned any of my calls, or emails. I just didn't know what to do to fix it.

It was mid-January when I suddenly realized that I hadn't been to see Quincy since Christmas Eve.

When I finally went to see Quincy, he was all smiles.

"Guess what!"

"You didn't get boinked in the shower?" I asked, and he slugged me playfully.

"Not yet…but remember those poems?"

"I still have them," I said defensively.

"Good, because someday they may be worth money," he said, leaning back. He smiled coyly.

"What are you talking about?"

"Darius Washington," he replied.

"Who?"

"The Vertical Poet."

"Huh?"

"Bantam."

"The book people? Okay… and?" I scrunched my eyebrows at him.

"A man by the name of Darius T. Washington submitted a collection of poetry to a Bantam representative. The only contact Mr. Darius had was his e-mail."

"Back the truck up!" I felt as though I was even farther from understanding.

"An e-mail was returned to Mr. Washington. It said, I don't know who you are, or where you are. But you need to contact me. I see great potential in you."

"Go on!" I urged.

"Darius T. Washington was my grandfather."

"Your grandfather sent in your poetry? But…wait…he's dead," I said, still confused. Then it hit me.

"You are Darius Washington?" I cried. "You used his name?"

"I could hardly believe it myself. I just didn't want to use my name, you know, in case he'd seen my face on the news or something. Tami, he wants me to contact him. I checked his credentials on the net, too. He's legit."

"Have you contacted him?"

"Surrounded by these four gray walls?" he asked, suddenly bitter.

"I'll be your secretary. I'll take care of it. I'm so damn proud of you, Quincy. I could scream. You've always been creative. You just chose to use your powers for evil."

"I love you. You know that?" he asked softly.

"I love you, too, Q."

A special and somewhat magical moment passed between us. Our eyes connected, and there is no other way to explain it, other than our souls also connected.

"What's that?" he asked. The tone changed quickly. His eyebrows furrowed. There was tension, anger, and suspicion in his voice. "What's that on your finger?"

"Oh…I forgot to tell you. I meant…to." The end of my sentence trailed off as he stood up. He walked directly to the door and without looking back, left.

❤❤❤

If only I had known then that in only a few days all of our lives would be changed.

My mother called one morning as I was on my way to work. She was crying. Without hesitating I turned down a side street, back toward the Bronx.

Was the cancer back?

"Mom? I can't understand you," I cried. She continued to blubber incoherently. My heart sank. Something had to be terribly wrong.

"Come!" she managed to spit out, and then I heard the phone drop. I drove faster than I should have dared. Twice I almost rear-ended someone and once I thought I had hit a cat. I looked in my rearview mirror horrified, but the cat sauntered slowly across the street. A black cat. Bad luck.

When I pulled up in front of my mother's house, the door was wide open. I ran inside, screaming her name. There was no response. The house was empty. The phone was back on the hook. Had someone been there? I wondered, possibly abducted her?

I picked up the phone to call the police, and then decided to check on Miss Dee. Miss Dee's door was wide open. The phone was off the hook in the hall downstairs. A fresh wave of panic washed over me.

I heard sobbing from upstairs. I raced up the stairs, tripping over my own feet. The first bedroom door on the right was open. I saw them. The old, light-skinned black woman, with salt-and-pepper hair. Her hair was pulled tightly back into a bun. She sat on the side of the bed. One of her breasts was gone, but she considered herself too old to care. Her face was flushed. Tears ran down her cheeks. She held the hand of her life-long best friend, Denise Patterson, also known as Miss Dee. I could tell just by looking at Miss Dee that she had been gone a long time. Perhaps the evening before when she and my mother had parted. The woman in the bed looked as peaceful in death as she had as a young mother tossing a ball with her son, and the little girl next door.

"Mom," I whispered. She turned to look at me, as if to say, *"Bring her back, baby. Please. I need her!"* And her composure fell, and she bent over to wrap her arms around Miss Dee's midsection.

Twenty Two

Quincy took it hard. I knew he would. He blamed himself. When I told him she had died in her sleep, peacefully, he didn't seem to believe me. I knew he wanted to cry. I could feel it. But he refused. I had told him as gently as possible. He wished I had been bringing good news about Bantam.

Ty, Trevor and I made the necessary arrangements. My mother was absolutely distraught, and could not help.

The funeral was exactly seven days after her death. Ty and Trevor scheduled it for Tuesday afternoon. On Saturday and Sunday I went to see Quincy. Each time, however, I was informed by the guards that he was accepting no visitors.

My mother insisted that people had different ways of grieving, and she was right. It was so difficult to accept that, when you are the one being rebuffed.

Marcus arranged an order that allowed Quincy to attend the funeral. There would be officers in attendance in plain clothes. He would be free of handcuffs.

One of Quincy's aunts arranged the same thing for his brother who was in a North Dakota prison. Jamil would be in handcuffs and supervised by uniformed officers. I was so disappointed when I heard he would be cuffed. That was definitely not how Miss Dee would have planned her going-home ceremony.

The night before the funeral, I found myself lying on my bed, with photo albums filled with pictures. Pictures that I shouldn't have been looking at during those times. They were pictures from when I was a child. They starred Quincy with a great big smile. Me with a gap-toothed grin. There was one of Miss Dee in her garden wearing a straw hat and smiling warmly. When I closed my eyes, I could hear her call across the yard to my mother. I remembered her barbecuing for her and Jamil. Quincy stood at the window upstairs on punishment. She laughed extra hard and extra loud, so he knew exactly what he was missing. That must have been when we were six and Jamil was seventeen. The year after, Jamil was hardly around. Miss Dee would cuss about him coming and going. *"Where you goin', boy? Does it look to you like I'm running some sort of soup kitchen heah? Don't grin, I ain't funnin'. This is the last time you set foot through these doors,"* she would yell. Jamil would kiss her, and say, "hey ma!" And then in a few days he would leave again.

He and Quincy never really got along in those days. Although, my mother said when he was younger, Jamil use to take Quincy everywhere with him. He was always under foot. One day, as I sat just inside the porch door, I overheard Mom and Miss Dee in a discussion I had no business listening to. Jamil had come in the night, and stolen all of Miss Dee's precious jewels. She had kept her wedding ring in a small locked box. He had taken that, too. He also had taken fifty-two dollars and thirty-five cents from her purse. Finally, she tearfully explained how she had immediately gone rushing downstairs to the sitting room fearful her great-grandmother's silver was also gone. And, of course it was. After that, Jamil never came or went again.

In the church I sat with my mother and Quincy. He said less than two words to me. When I began to cry, he reached over and gripped my hand. He clung to me so tightly, his despair seemed to leak off his skin and right into mine.

The church was filled with people we didn't even know. I guess that is the nature of things; people come to honor you in death, with feelings of guilt for not making time while you were alive.

I sat, hearing none of the minister's words. I kept thinking, just a few days ago, she was here. Now she was not. In my heart where God lay, I suddenly began to doubt His existence. What if she really was nowhere right now? Her body was simply going to be put into a box in the earth. The bugs would eventually eat through the box until nothing was left. No matter how expensive a box we bought, unless it were made of metal, she would become a meal for countless insects. What if that were the truth? If there were no heaven how the hell was I going to accept this? One day she was here, and the next day she wasn't. I was filled with overwhelming sadness, thoughts that consumed me, and scary emotions that were questioning my belief in God. Biting my lip was all I could do to not burst into an uncontrollable system of tears.

Marcus sat in the pew beside us, with Ty and his father. I didn't even look back, but I knew that Jamil and his police officers were sitting in the back of the church. Quincy did not falter. He did not shed a tear. He sat with his jaw clenched tightly, and even then I thought of how attractive he was. Miss Dee had made beautiful children.

At the gravesite, I felt torn. Quincy was on one side. Ty was on the other. I wanted to take Quincy's hand as the casket was being lowered. I wanted to tell him to cry. I wanted to put my arms around him. He stood so rigidly, watching intently as the casket was being lowered. It was as if he was trying to commit the events to memory.

Jamil was on the other side of the plot. He, like Quincy, had been permitted to wear a suit. He looked so much older I was shocked at first. He kept his face down and seemed to slump over with guilt.

The casket was lowered slowly. And fittingly, it began to drizzle.

At one point Jamil and I made eye contact. It was clear he remembered me. He broke our gaze quickly, and seemed to slump further. But, I had seen it. Guilt, remorse, regret. Without him speaking, I knew he was sorry things had worked out the way they had. I was surprised to find pity for him in my heart. Who am I to judge anyway? I don't know him. I don't even know what he did to land him in jail.

"Are you all right?" Ty whispered in my ear, and I nodded.

"I'm gonna help your mother to the car," he said. I was so glad he was there. He rubbed my shoulder before departing.

"Quincy, I'll be in my car, if you need a minute," Marcus said, cutting through the crowds that were departing. Quincy simply nodded. I gave Marcus a thankful smile and he winked at me. Then I turned to Quincy, wanting to throw my arms around him.

"Quincy...," I began, but before I could finish, there was a voice that interrupted us.

"Quincy. Can I talk to you for a moment?" It was Jamil, and he was standing behind me. He appeared to loom over us, his height a definite advantage. His officers stood about three feet back. Quincy looked up at him and then back to me. His face was blank.

"No!" Quincy replied. I was shocked and a little hurt.

"I just wanna say a few things to you, man. I know we haven't been close...," Jamil continued.

"You didn't hear me or what? I don't want to talk to you. Get lost!" Quincy snapped. This time he looked at Jamil with a steely, challenging gaze.

My heart leapt into my chest. "Quincy," I protested.

"Stay out of this!" he ordered. He walked away leaving Jamil and I behind.

Jamil looked at me as if to apologize. Had he reformed? How long was he even going to be there? I wanted him to have another chance.

"I'm sorry," I whispered, and turned to leave. Then I paused.

"She forgave you, Jamil. She really really loved you," I said to him. I thought maybe that's what he wanted to hear because a tear fell from his eye and onto his cheek. He looked meekly at me and forced a smile. I turned to catch up to Quincy who was walking to the car with the officers.

"Quincy," I called. "Quincy, wait." He froze. It was as though he didn't really want to wait, but felt he owed it to me. He did not turn around.

"Why won't you see me?" I asked him, when I reached his side. He looked down at me in that way that makes me feel like I am his property or something. I don't know exactly how he does it, but he does, and I despise that look

"I've been busy."

"In jail?" I cried. "Too busy for visitors?"

"I need time," he said. I groaned.

"I wish you would talk to me. You'll feel better. I promise," I said.

"Maybe. Maybe not!" He left me standing there. I felt like I wanted to cry. Finally I did. When I looked up, I saw Ty standing beside the car on the road. He stared at me for a moment, looking puzzled. Then he beckoned me over. My wet hair began to cling to my face, and I brushed furiously at it, feeling disappointed, upset and frustrated.

♥♥♥

I went twice a week for the rest of the month. Quincy still refused to see me. I kept telling myself that he would come around. Marcus assured me he was all right, but Quincy had not discussed with him when he might be willing to see me.

Mom appeared to be doing okay. But, occasionally I would catch her with a very lost, reminiscent look in her eyes. Then she'd snap out of it, as though it hadn't even happened.

Her disposition improved greatly, when just a few weeks later, our visit to the doctor revealed good news. For the time being, there was no cancer in her body. With careful monitoring, he thought she would make a full recovery.

In the middle of February, Quincy finally came out to see me. He shook his head as he sat down.

"You just don't give up, do you?"

I ignored his comment.

"How have you been?" he asked. I felt like laughing hysterically. I felt like screaming. He had been ignoring me. Why did he care how I was?

Instead, I said, "I've been all right. How are you?"

"Fine! Under the circumstances. I'm thinking about applying for another year in here," he replied. "Thanks for the birthday gift."

"How's the book?" I had dropped off a book of poetry for his birthday.

"Nowhere near mine!" he said without any emotion.

"I called that guy for you. He agreed to put a file on hold until you return from your volunteer work in the Yucatan," I told him. For a moment he said nothing, then finally he smirked.

"The Yucatan, huh?"

"It was the first place that came to mind."

"Three months until the trial," he told me. I nodded. He had not fallen apart in jail as I thought he might have.

"I have a feeling about Marcus. I just know that things will work out. That kid isn't dead. He's paralyzed, I think. But, he didn't die. That's good news. You won't be in here past the trial," I said.

He looked at me as though he wished he could think the same way. Then there was a silence so loud you could hear a pin drop. In his face there were so many unchartered emotions, I could barely sit there and look at him.

"You have to stop this!" I whispered.

"What?"

"Punishing yourself." I reached across the table to take his hand. I just wanted to be there for him, to be his friend, let him know that I was there for him.

I was hurting, too, but I had Ty and my mother to talk to. There he had no one.

He turned my hands over in his and seemed to be examining them. He flipped my left hand over, and stared at the ring on my finger. His eyes became sad, his brows furrowed deeply. I knew he was thinking. You could fill your pockets with the tension.

"Aunt Ruth's daughter, Julia, used to visit," he began. He spoke so softly, that I had to read his lips to fully comprehend.

I tried to look as encouraging as possible.

"When we were little, Aunt Ruth would drop her off sometimes and she would play with us on the weekends. She and I were around the same age. She was the only little girl, other than you, that I would play with. I remember one day we were playing hide and seek in the backyard. I was trying to find her. I must have looked, and called her name for ten minutes. Then I gave up, and abandoned the search for a cartoon on television. Half an hour later I heard muffled screams. Mom was outside. I thought I knew where the screams were coming from. So, I went to look for Julia. She was in the den. In the dark storage closet I found her. She was under Jamil. He must have been fifteen, and she was seven. Poor kid. I never told anyone. I doubt she ever did, either. I didn't know what to do. I didn't really know what he was doing. I was so confused. He had his hand over her mouth and she just kept making those same desperate attempts at screaming. I just walked away. After that, she never came back. We never saw her again for any of the family meetings, or…well…for anything really.

"To this day, I think I should have done something or at least said something. But I can't stand him. Even if he did wanna talk to me, I can't forget that. I can't forget any of it. He's where he belongs, Tamara. And I know you thought maybe he was different. I could see it in your eyes at the funeral, but he hasn't changed. I used to blame myself. I thought if I'd just kept searching, he wouldn't have found her before I had. I just imagine sometimes what that did to her. I wish we had never played hide and seek. I wish that Jamil had never found her. I wish he was dead. I can never ever forgive him for what he did."

"It wasn't your fault. You were a little boy," I told him. He nodded.

"Quincy…," I began. He stood up. I knew that was all he was willing to share for one day.

"I'll see you later," I whispered. He pursed his lips, and then took a step toward me. He pulled me to my feet and hugged me. I hugged him from the bottom of my heart. I couldn't change the past, but I could be here for him in the future. I wanted him to know that.

He pulled away, brushed my cheek with his hand and then walked from the room.

Twenty Three

"You know what, it's not that I don't want Brick to see his son. But the damn guy has been in jail all this time. I know he's out, and doing the same shit he did to land himself in there in the first place. I just don't trust him with Keegan," Liv said. She was beyond perplexed. She had been holding the same piece of fettuccine wound around her fork for the past five minutes. She occasionally used it to help narrate her story.

It was driving me friggin' nuts.

"Eat it!" Traci snapped suddenly. I looked at her, shocked.

"I'm sorry, Liv, you've been holding that damn piece of pasta for a year. Eat the damn thing!"

Olivia looked at her fork and then burst into laughter

"Liv, Brick hasn't sent cards, he hasn't called, he hasn't even asked to see Keegan. I don't think you should let him take him," I pointed out.

"It's worse than that. He sent a letter from his damn lawyer," Olivia said angrily.

"They are not going to give him Keegan. How would that look to a judge? What will he say? '*I was in jail for years, but suddenly I have decided that I am a model father*'?" Traci asked.

I smiled to myself. The smile disappeared from my face as I looked around the empty table. This had been my attempt at a

Sunday lunch reconciliation. Only three of us were interested in fixing this. Daeshondra claimed she was sick. As she was hanging up the phone, she coughed rather dryly for added effect. Jaclyn had said it was Sunday; she would be meeting some of the wives of the church after the service. Precious had simply told me she did not want to get caught up in all this drama. Shan was still not returning my calls or answering the phone. Devora said she was going through a divorce, and this was no time for friends. It hadn't made much sense to me. I had been about to protest that I had been there for her, and I was not to be put into the middle of things, then I changed my mind and hung up.

I realized as I drove home, things would never be quite the same again. We were, in a sense, closing a very monumental chapter of our lives. There was a sadness so deep, not even my faith could find the bottom as it sank within me.

Ty and I went to Dim Sum's for an early dinner. He and I were laughing at the prospect of running away to elope, when I got the shock of my life. The ex-boyfriend who had received a broken nose as my parting gift walked up to our table. He grinned foolishly at me.

"Tamara Jones," he said declaratively.

What? Had I not known my own name?

"Dalyle Wesley," I said and snickered.

I was surprised that he was actually willing to acknowledge me. His nose had a crooked appearance to it.

"How are you?" he asked. He looked the same. Nothing had changed with the exception of a long scar that stretched from his left eyebrow to his left ear. I suspected it was the result of a bar brawl. He had been notorious for those. Either that or some other unimpressed girlfriend had done it. I hoped for the latter. I noticed he was still mildly attractive, but I wasn't interested.

"Dalyle, I have never been better. Thanks for asking. How have you been?" I looked over at Ty, who sat with a smug look on his face. It was one of those contented looks, where you know more about someone than they think you know. He certainly knew who Dalyle was.

"I've been good. Miss ya, though," he added.

Ty began to cough. I looked at him concerned, but the look he gave me was pure amusement.

"Dalyle, this is my fiancé, Tyrone. Ty, this is Dalyle." Dalyle shook his hand.

"Why don't you join us for a few moments?" Ty suggested with a quick *okay* glance toward me. I ran my leg up the side of his leg under the table.

Dalyle looked to the rear of the restaurant for a moment. He decided to sit down.

"You here with someone?" Ty asked him.

"Some ho. But she's not so smart. I'm sure she won't realize I'm gone for a few minutes," he replied. He sat in the chair between Ty and me. I realized then that things hadn't changed one bit. Every time we went out, Dalyle would get a page, tell me he would be back, and then be gone for fifteen minutes or so. Once I just left him in the restaurant. That was in the beginning of our relationship. He had girls, he drank, he smoked up, and he cheated. He was so messed up. I had tried to end it so many times. When I tried to leave, he would beg and plead. He hit me once. The second time he hit me was my fault, because I should have left the first time. It all came flooding back to me as I watched him talking to Ty.

The moment that broke my back was vivid in my memory. It happened at Monty's on a Saturday night. I had just started at Bronx West, and had finished up a week of late nights trying to perfect things after they had been tasked to me. Dalyle had offered to take me out Saturday night to wind down. First I arrived late, and he was mad. Then there was the fact that he had been drinking since he woke up at twelve. When I insisted on driving because he was drunk, we had gotten into yet another fight. When I turned to go back up to my apartment, he had finally given in and followed me to my car. In the car we fought about everything. He accused me of cheating on him that week instead of working. Eventually, I suggested that perhaps he was the one that was doing the cheating. He called me a ho, which prompted another argument about his lack of respect.

At the club he had tried to jump the line, but was ridiculed by the bouncer who told him to take a hike. I left our spot in the back of the line to stop him from pissing the bouncer off further, and the bouncer took a liking to me, and decided to let us in. Dalyle had stood up to his full five nine, as though it was his doing so that got us in. I remember the bouncer had said to him, "Not on account of you, little man; on account of the pretty lady." This riled Dalyle up while we were in the club. I couldn't wipe the smile off my face, and he kept glaring at me.

The club was absolutely packed. We were there for a half hour when Dalyle said he was going to get a drink and wanted to know what I wanted. I told him to bring me a Cosmopolitan. I stood there for a half hour. When he didn't return, I went to find him. He was standing in front of the ladies room talking to some girl with a horrendous weave. Her face looked magic-markered. I walked back to our spot without saying anything to him. He returned a half-hour later with a Malibu pineapple. I assumed he had not only forgotten my drink, but had bought that drink for some other woman who didn't accept it or something. I glared at him for a long while, then told him the drink wasn't the right one. He told me to be thankful that I had a drink at all. When I asked him what took so long, he told me the line was long. He then asked me what the hell my problem was. I told him he was my problem. Then I asked him about the girl. I asked him if he had stuck it to her in the corner. He had the nerve to tell me it took him longer than a minute. Nowhere near the truth. I turned to leave. He grabbed my arm, and gripped it unbelievably tight. The people around us became alarmed. A very large, very thick man took a few paces toward us. I turned back to Dalyle and stared him down. He refused to let go. I knew then it was put up or get out. Through clenched teeth I told him to let me go. When he didn't, I took my glass of Malibu Pineapple and jammed it on the bridge of his nose. The glass seemed to shatter into a million pieces in slow motion. I didn't even wait to see what would happen. I simply walked away. I heard later that I'd broken his nose. He had told people I had simply snapped and that was why he broke up with me. I didn't care by that point.

Now here he was, and my beautiful fiancé was talking to him like they were old friends. I felt like getting up to tell the girl he was with, who he really was. But I knew she would have to find out herself, just like I had.

Ty brushed his leg up and down mine. It was a pleasant reminder that I was no longer where I used to be. I had come a long way. It felt good.

"It was nice meeting you, man. You take care," Ty said to Dalyle.

Dalyle seemed thrown for a second, then took the hint that he was being dismissed. He went to kiss my hand, but I pulled it back.

"Take care, Dalyle," I said.

He smiled at me, then walked away.

"Quite the character," Ty told me. "Are you all right?"

"Yeah. It was just a real shock to see him after so long. All I have are bad memories of him. I don't wanna know him at all."

"Then we won't," he said smiling. "How about a walk in Central Park?" I looked at my half-eaten piece of chocolate cake.

"You bet! Gotta finish my cake, though," I replied. When I looked up at him, he reached across the table and ran the back of his hand gently across my cheek. He smiled when I stopped chewing and gazed at him.

"I wouldn't dream of separating you from cake."

❤❤❤

"I'm not a bad person," Quincy said.

"I know."

"Well, not all the time," he said, and then snickered. "Just when I have nowhere to concentrate my energy."

"Quincy, you are twenty-six years old. This is supposed to come naturally by now."

He smiled. His features then took on a very troubled, serious look.

"I miss her," he whispered.

"I know."

Quincy opened up over the next few weeks, in ways I never thought possible. I realized that he was more afraid of life than he dared to admit. I realized also that I loved him. I loved him as though he and I were really blood relatives.

Twenty Four

"I have a fabulous idea," Ty whispered. I was sitting at the kitchen table reading over some notes from work. Ty had been fixing the window in the guestroom.

"What's that?" I asked and looked up absentmindedly.

My face broke into a smile. He was wearing his boxer briefs. I wanted to eat him alive. I loved seeing him in his underwear. He looked like an underwear model. He stood in the shadow of the late-afternoon sun, like a Calvin Klein ad. I sat at the table, sheltered from that same sun, feeling unbelievably weak all over. God! It felt good.

"You're fixing the window naked?"

"It's hot!" he replied.

"It's April. It's spring," I protested. He turned and flexed his body into a muscle pose. He was so sexy. He needed to stop!

"It feels like summer in here. Why don't you get naked with me?"

"Don't tempt me now."

"That's the plan," he whispered. Before I could protest he was behind me, massaging my shoulders and my neck. Four seconds flat, and I was out of my shirt. Then we were on the kitchen floor, writhing underneath each other.

"What was your idea?" I whispered breathlessly.

"That we should go somewhere this evening."

"Where do you want to go?"

"No idea. As long as it's with you, I'm happy," he said. But then we were too out of breath to say much more than "oh yeah! Oh baby…" And when we were all done, he asked, "And?"

"Best! Best! Best!" I replied as he collapsed on the floor.

No matter how much money anyone had, Quincy had spent a year of his life in jail. It was a year that he was never getting back. All the money I had spent on a lawyer, hadn't made a difference in the short term. I banished the thoughts as he came through the door.

"You again," he said, smiling.

"It's only me!"

"You look nice. Where you off to?" he asked. I looked at the jean dress I was wearing, realizing for the first time that I looked sensational!

"Nowhere special."

He looked at me as though knowing what I was going to say next.

"Are you going *nowhere* special with Tyrone?"

"Bravo, Quincy, for the first time you have called him by his name. Yes, with Tyrone." I reached across the table to poke him in the arm. He jumped back as if my touch burnt.

"Don't get all violent on me now, girl."

"Violent? I am not the one who burnt and melted Barbie's dream house when we were six," I protested, my voice dripping with sarcasm.

"You just can't let it go, can you? Why don't you go and burn down my house. Will that make you feel better?" he asked, chuckling.

"You don't have a house anymore, Q. Otherwise, I might," I said cockily.

"Where y'all goin?"

"We're meeting some friends. Out in the country. We need to breathe clean air for a few hours," I replied.

Quincy nodded with a strange look on his face.

"What?" I asked.

"I didn't say anything."

"No! But you have that look," I insisted.

"What look would that be?"

"The 'I'm lost in thought' *look*. 'I'm thinking of saying something' *look*."

"You don't want to hear it," he told me.

"How are you gonna tell me what I want to hear?" I snapped. "Spill."

"Well, I was thinking. The worst feeling in the world is to watch someone you love, love someone else," he said softly, and then he met my eyes. He looked at me as though he was looking through me.

"Why would you be thinking that all of a sudden?"

"No reason," he replied.

"You have to have some reason."

"None whatsoever!" he said absentmindedly, and then looked away. "Almost done here." He looked around the visitors room.

"What? Are you gonna miss it?"

"Maybe," he replied jokingly.

"Who are you in love with?"

"I'm not sure I am."

"Then why'd you say it?"

"Because I was thinking it."

"Must have had a reason."

"Not necessarily."

"Of course, or you wouldn't have said it. Who is it?"

"She's not ready to hear it."

"How's she supposed to be ready, if you don't tell her?"

"Well, that's counter-productive, Tamara." He paused. "It'd be best if she knew when she was willing to accept it. If she's not, then there's no point."

He was right. I wasn't ready to hear it, was I? Me? Shit! Was he telling me that he might be in love with me? The way that I had been carrying on, I had been subconsciously urging him onward. I had Ty. I couldn't sit there and encourage it.

"I have something for you," he said, when the guard gave us the signal.

Time was up. Quincy stood up and handed me an envelope from his pocket. "Don't read it until you are ready. Even if it's three years from now."

"I don't know if I will ever be ready. Ty is very much in love with me," I told him. He nodded indifferently. I wasn't sure he felt indifferent, however. He definitely had a vested interest in this.

"He's in love with you? What about you being in love with him?" he asked.

"Well, obviously, I mean me, too."

"Obviously!" he agreed sarcastically.

Then we parted ways.

❤❤❤

During the car ride out to Billings Bridge, I was completely lost in thought—not so much that Ty noticed. He was so excited for me to meet his best friend Christopher and his wife, Dayanara. But the conversation I'd had with Quincy was on rewind in my head. I wanted it out. The letter was safely tucked away in my purse.

"Baby, you hungry?" Ty asked. "We can stop at the next town and get a bite to eat."

"Not really. You wanna get something, though?"

"Naw! I'll wait till supper," he said. "And then dessert." He gave me a look, which meant I would be dessert. I was perfectly all right with that.

"What did you do this morning?" he asked out of the blue.

"Not much. Had a few things to look over for work. Read a little. Called Devora and Jaclyn, but they didn't pick up."

"You didn't leave home?" he asked. "You missed the big accident over by the heliport. There must have been about fifteen cars involved in it. I missed it by maybe ten minutes."

Actually I had seen the accident. I was stuck in it for almost an hour. But, for some reason I did not mention it.

Christopher was a tall, thick, attractive white man. He had dark, beautiful hair and blue eyes. His wife, Dayanara, was stunning. Her hair was jet black, and cascaded in waves down her back. She was tall and shapely, with flawless skin. She looked Greek or Roman, sort of like one of those mythological goddesses. They stood on the front step side by side as we pulled up.

Christopher was a successful stockbroker, and used to commute over an hour from Billings Bridge to New York each day to work. Ty explained that he made so much money now that he could afford to work from home. He could make the trip once a week if absolutely necessary.

As I closed the car door the sense of peace hit me instantly. There were birds chirping, a wet dewy smell, and the pleasant, wet smell that accompanies spring blossoms. In the city we never experienced this. You heard cars honking and kids screaming. You smelled smoke and garbage. If it wasn't for the thawing of the snow and the increase in rain instead of snow, we would not know it was spring.

Their house was beautiful, set far back from a long winding driveway. They had what appeared to be an infinite amount of land. In fact, their house looked as though it had simply been placed amongst a beautiful backdrop of rolling hills and thick green foliage. There was a splash of color against the house, as flowers began to bloom. Was it possible that spring came sooner in the country?

"Coming?" Ty asked, turning to look back at me. I simply stood staring at my surroundings. I closed the car door and went to join him.

"It is so nice to finally meet you. After all you are the woman who will be marrying my best friend," Christopher said and reached for my hand. I shook amiably. His wife was introduced to me, and I smiled at her, admiring her beauty. She was even more beautiful than Jaclyn. I had never really met anyone who was. My thoughts about her Greek background were confirmed when she commented on my charming outfit. She had a distinctly Mediterranean accent.

After dinner, Chris and Ty went for a walk outside. Dayanara and I sat in the den making polite conversation. However, just after her third drink her tongue became a little loose, she unbuttoned the top button on her blouse and looked even more relaxed.

"You two make a good couple, Tamara."

"Oh…thanks. We um…we get along really well. We don't fight," I told her. She had caught me off guard. "You and Chris, too."

"No…we fight! We fight about what day to wash the clothes. We fight about whether to name our children Jack or Jill. We fight about fighting sometimes. Let me tell you, marriage is not what it is cracked up to be. I can't stand the way he sleeps, the way he leaves the toilet seat up. I can't stand anything about him actually."

"Oh…I'm sorry."

"You don't have to be sorry. I am sorry. I am the one who said yes. I left the love of my life to say yes. You have no idea how I wish I hadn't done that."

"Why did you say yes to him."

"My family is very religious. Old World Christian Eastern Orthodox. We…"—she began to slur her words—"…are a proud people. The love of my life would have been a disgrace on my entire family. I would have been disinherited and cast out of my family. Then along came this nice American boy, his name was Christopher. One of his parents was Greek, and he was a Christian. When he asked me to marry him, I thought…this can't be that bad."

I felt sorry for her. She was falling apart right in front of me. Here I was technically still a stranger. I wondered how often she got to talk with anyone else. Here she was living in the country, far away from absolutely everything. How quick I had been to elevate her life out here and put down my busy life in the city.

"It's bad! I don't love him. In fact, I don't even like him. I think he is arrogant. He is a fool."

"What will you do?"

"I can't do anything. I'm stuck. I'm locked in. If I divorce him, my family will kill me. I mean that literally."

"And the love of your life? What happened to him?" I queried.

"*She*…killed herself."

Twenty Five

My mother and I were sitting right behind Quincy and Marcus in the section where his family should be. I had never been so nervous in my life. The prosecution had so far presented evidence that Quincy was the only person laying the blows. The prosecution had two sorry little mofos testify that they saw Quincy kicking the kid. One of them could only say he saw him from the back. The other one saw him from a window. That was the best they had.

And then there was the videotape. The damning videotape where Quincy was seen kicking the kid. The kid who got beat up was sitting with his lawyer. He was in a wheelchair. He still looked pretty jacked up. One of his eyes was permanently closed. His legs looked lifeless and thin.

I knew in the depths of my heart that Quincy had not messed up that kid Antony like that. Sometimes I wondered how all of this looked to everyone else. The kid had no clue who had beat the shit out of him. He said so when he got on the stand. His story was that he was doing some coke in the back of the house. Some guy named Lou was supposed to be at that party. He owed Lou upward of four grand for something he had sold for him. So the kid, Antony, said to his friend, they had to split. He explained that if they ran into Lou, Lou was gonna roll him right there. On their way out to their car, some guy picked a fight with Antony. It was someone he had never seen before. But he was certain it wasn't Quincy. It was some white dude. The dude was in the courtroom, and the prosecutor made him point to the guy. The white guy nodded his head.

I was shocked. The guy who started the damn thing was reformed in a nice blue suit and acting as a witness for the very same kid he started a fight with? Antony continued, explaining that he and his friend were up against this guy they didn't know, and some other guy. But he was looking at them both when suddenly he received a blow on the back of the head. That was all he could remember.

The prosecution had to prove that Quincy was the one that hit him in the back of the head. The prosecutor was this bald, little, fat man. He could not pinpoint when Quincy came into the picture. In fact, he couldn't make a clear connection with Quincy and the victim. What he did know was that Quincy was on the tape throwing punches and kicking the victim and they had witnesses to prove it. He spoke about the troubled past of the witnesses, but stated they had been clean from the time of the incident. Quincy, he pointed out, at the time of arrest, had tested positive for drugs in his system. Quincy also had a record, where both the witnesses did not.

Then the prosecution called three of Antony's family members. They talked about how Antony was before he had been injured, and how his life had changed. I felt sorry for the kid, but I kept thinking, *don't forget he was in the house, smoking crack*. And, he owed some guy a couple thousand dollars. How much more did he owe other people?

The following day, things went smoothly. Marcus called Trey,

Shoop and Zel to the stand. They managed to show up completely sober. They were extremely convincing when they said Q had nothing to do with it. But, at one point, Marcus had to stop Shoop.

"Mr. Lewis, can you repeat that part again. A fight?"

"Yeah, I got out to the yard late, you know. Cuz I was downstairs, and I see Quincy talking up some G. She was real fine, so I gave him a minute. Then finally, I just went up and slapped him on the back, yo! You know, trying to get a lil' introduction to this piece of ass. Anyway, turns out, it wasn't Q. It was some guy, wearin' his jacket. So, I felt dumb, you know? But, the guy was trippin', asked if I was tryna start something. I backed up...I wasn't with that! I went to juvie when I was sixteen, bro. I wasn't doin' that again."

"So, this *other* guy, was wearing the same jacket as Quincy you said?" Marcus asked.

Shoop looked at him as though he were a fool. "Didn't you just hear me say that?" Even though Shoop didn't understand yet, I understood the implications clearly.

When they played the tape, and Marcus was cross-examining one of the police officers that had processed the case, Marcus asked, "Can you see what kind of shoes those are? I can't see really clearly."

The police officer leaned forward, squinted his eyes. After a moment, he said, "They're Nikes."

"Oh! Okay, thank you! Wait...how do you know that?" Marcus asked.

"The swoosh on the back!"

"Thank you," Marcus said, and then faced the jury. "This is an important note for later. The person kicking the victim wore white Nikes. As I'm sure you all can agree. Particularly because their witness has perfect vision. After all, he saw the defendant *all* the way from the window of the house." The jury and most of the audience looked puzzled.

"Isn't that right?" he asked the police officer, who nodded confused.

Marcus called Quincy's Aunt Ruth who spoke kindly of him. Marcus decided at the very last minute to put Quincy on the stand.

He was nervous as he took that oath. I just kept praying he could compose himself. But even his voice shook. So, on May 23, Marcus drove his point home.

The videotape had been tampered with. Marcus had had the tape examined by an expert, who took the stand and explained the situation. There was editing before the beating and after the beating. He assumed it was the owner of the videotape who had done it, because it was clearly recorded over by a regular VCR. The snow that ran across the screen before and after the beating was the evidence he was certain would clear Quincy. The judge had the tape examined, and then ruled that the tape was no longer admissible in court. It was struck from the list of evidence. My mother was squeezing my hand so tightly when this was revealed, all I could do was squeeze back so as not to lose circulation.

Then, there was the evidence that wrapped the case. The blood they found on Quincy's shoes was a very big part of the prosecution's argument. Marcus insisted that only proved that Quincy was there. He and his friends had already admitted that. Point taken. Not only that, but he was jumping the fence when the cops arrived. The fence was in the backyard. There was blood all over the backyard, from the beating. In fact, if they tested the blood on any of the other individuals' shoes, they would find it also matched the victims. The two guys that had testified to seeing

Quincy laying punches also had blood on their shoes. It was clear in the police report. This also meant their story of being nowhere near the fight, watching from windows was untrue. What the prosecution could not produce was any DNA evidence belonging to the victim on Quincy's shoes.

Marcus noted that Quincy's shoes were labeled in the police report at the time of processing as white-and-black Tevas. Marcus turned on the projector which displayed clearly against the white wall. The screen showed a picture in the basement of the party. There was a blur in the top corner that was probably a finger. It was also a bit lopsided. The photo had been blown up to forty times its size. It showed two men in the picture. Both of them were black. Both of them had on the exact same jacket. Quincy was the one across the room sitting against the bar with Zel and Shoop. Then the other fellow was leaving through the door with a girl. Marcus had been alluding to this exact same jacket through-out the entire proceedings. Now, he pulled it together for every-one else. There was a sudden look of realization on Quincy's face. He turned to look at me. I figured it was because he had remem-bered seeing a guy wearing the exact same jacket.

Tension mounted.

Marcus said the evidence was handled poorly. He said the prosecution had overlooked a few crucial points to prove their case. The other guy in the photo was also wearing white sneakers. They were Nikes. "The videotape is no longer admissible, but you'll do well to remember seeing for yourselves, the white Nikes that were on the feet of the aggressor. Those were not the shoes that the police reported my defendant wearing. There's a good reason for that. Because, he wasn't wearing Nikes. He wore Tevas. Meaning, he was not the one involved in the fight. He simply ran through the backyard and stepped in some blood on the way out. He ran, just like the rest of the men who testified today. Unfortunately, he was the only one wrongfully accused." Part way through his speech the prosecutor had objected because the tape was inadmissible. Marcus was on a roll, however, and made his point before the judge chided him.

The minute he finished, I stood up and began to cheer. I wasn't the only one standing and cheering. The judge banged on his gavel, but it only made me clap louder. I could not sit down. Quincy swiveled around in his chair and calmly looked at me, his eyes full of tears.

"Thank you," he whispered.

I smiled broadly.

"It was nothing!"

Twenty Six

"You're not yourself. What's up?" Ty asked.

"Nothing!"

"Don't say 'nothing,' Tami. It's not 'nothing.' You haven't been yourself since we got back from the country. Talk to me," he said patiently.

I looked out the window, feeling broken and tired. Something was happening to me. I couldn't define it. I couldn't even locate it. Was it in my heart or in my head? It probably had something to do with the fact that Quincy was now living with me. I had offered my place until he got himself on his feet. The problem was that I hadn't told Ty. I had been avoiding the subject and dodging corners everytime I was faced with it. We had been standing at a hotdog stand downtown one afternoon. On the front page there had been an article about Quincy being wrongfully accused. Ty had not yet put together our connection, and I couldn't quite figure out how. Quincy was everywhere. If he had even spoken to Marcus he must know who he was defending. Had my Mom never mentioned the entire trial to Ty's Dad? But I had gotten myself so far into this secret, that I just knew it would look suspect if I brought it up now. I just kept hoping it would disappear, and we'd never have to discuss it.

"It's nothing," I insisted. We drove the rest of the way home in complete silence. I thought to myself, *I don't wanna be near him right now*. It's like when you have an argument with someone and you just want to be far away from them. That was how I felt, and that feeling made me want to cry. I couldn't even look his way for fear I would break down.

Outside my house we sat in the car. For five minutes we said nothing.

"Your mother told me about her surgery," he said.

Shit! I had meant to tell him about that.

"I was gonna tell you."

"Right! But this is a major thing. You should have told me. I should have been there to support you both. Tamara, I should have known," he said.

"I'm sorry. And I wanted to tell you. Honestly."

"The morning we left for Billings Bridge, what did you do?"

"Huh? I don't remember. Didn't you ask me that then?"

"No! You lied to me. What is Quincy to you?" he asked. This took my breath away. I thought I was gonna fall flat on my face. I was at a loss for words, actions, anything, and that seemed to make things worse.

"Why didn't you just tell me the truth? That he was who you were with? I thought we were great together. Good for each other, had no secrets, trusted each other. A future. I thought we were the Livingstons, and we were going to start a family," he mused. He was hurt, probably more hurt than I had ever seen him in all of our time together. He was acting as though he knew something more that I did not know. "You do love me, right? Because if you don't, say so."

"I do!" I told him.

"Really? Say it. Say, Ty, I love you."

"Why are you doing this?"

"Just say it!"

"You know I do!" I said angrily and between clenched teeth.

"You can't do it!" he said. He put his head down in his hands. His entire frame slumped over. I had never seen him like that before.

"I don't know why you're speaking to me like this!" I protested.

"You don't keep important things from someone you love."

"I know," I whispered. I wasn't sure what I was feeling right then. I didn't even really care about me. I knew he was in pain, and I was attempting to communicate my regrets to him the best way I knew possible. It just wasn't coming out like I wanted it to. No matter what I said, he was being hurt every time I opened my mouth. I felt backed against a wall.

"Why do you think you didn't tell me about Quentin?"

"Quincy."

"Whatever!" he mumbled. I blinked at his rejection.

"I don't know, Ty. I was...see, it's like this...I..." But I couldn't finish, because he started the car. He seemed so sad to me. He was angry and frustrated. I understood that it was my fault. I could feel this tugging, this yanking right where it would hurt the most. I could feel the tears, feel them, wanted them, but they weren't running yet. I guess in the back of my mind I knew then. I had known, felt it, could even sense it from him. But I couldn't force myself to react. Not that it mattered.

"Yeah?" he urged.

"He...he...was my friend. He lived next door."

"Where is he living now?"

"He...uh...with me," I whispered.

"That's why you don't let me up?"

"I was just waiting for the right time to tell you. I just wasn't sure how to do it. I thought you'd have a hard time accepting it."

"Tamara. I trusted you. I would have been willing to understand anything."

Okay, so now I knew. I wanted to move on. I wanted to move forward. I was certain that if this was ending right there, I was going to fall apart.

"So why the lies, the secrets? You can never tell me where you're going," he said. "I used to trust you. But, now I don't know who the hell you are. I thought maybe if I gave you time, everything would go away. But, it's getting worse."

"It's not going to get worse. It's going to get better."

"I thought that if I waited you would realize you did love me. I wanted you to really want to spend the rest of your life with me. I have given you ample opportunities to open up to me. You haven't. If it's all innocent, then why not just tell me the truth?"

"I'm telling you now."

"Do you love him?"

"NO!"

"Does he love you?"

"Ty...no. No, he doesn't. We are just friends. I helped him get out of jail. He was innocent...," I began, but he cut me off.

"No. I helped him get out. I gave you Marcus' number. Your fiancé got a man that is in love with you out of jail." He raised his voice. I looked at him shocked.

"No. He doesn't..."

He said nothing, but reached over to his glove compartment. When he flipped it open I wasn't sure what I was looking at. Then I saw it. The envelope that Quincy had given me. I realized then, I had forgotten all about it. Had it fallen out of my pocket?

"It was beside your seat in the car. A plain envelope. I didn't even know what it was or who it was for. But, then I read it. And, he does love you. I thought, if she does not love him back, this will work. But...you do love him. You lied to me about him, and I can see it in your face. You love him!"

I could think of nothing to say. I wanted to scream, or cry, or show some form of emotion other than shock. But, there was nothing there. I had dried up. I was empty.

"Why didn't you tell me the truth?" he asked.

"Because the truth will hurt you," I mumbled. I'm not sure why I said that. I do love him, so what kind of truth would hurt him? What did I mean?

"Get out of my car, please. I'm gonna leave because I love you. Because if I stay, I will say things that I will regret saying later," he said, trying not to cry. There is nothing worse than watching someone try not to cry. It always made me cry. Finally, the tears began to spill down my face.

"Nothing you say will make me think any less of you," I told him. I didn't want him to leave. I didn't want him to leave with me still loving him.

"Everything you've said has made me think less of you," he whispered. It stung. "I have loved you so much. Now I cannot trust you, and I don't think you will ever be able to love me as much as I love you. This is a guy that you've known since you were a child. And, you dated him. Let me guess. He was your first love. Your first, well...everything. And I understand that this is probably minor in the grand scheme of things. But not to me; I can't marry someone who has kept things from me. I also cannot marry a woman who may love someone else."

Even as he said that, I knew he was right. I had ruined something very special. I had broken something in him. I was regretful but that was not enough. I couldn't go back and take back the things that had happened. Nor could I take back the way I felt.

"Good luck!" he said, and didn't even turn to look at me. He reached over and pushed my door open. "Please don't call me. I think it's for the best!"

I got out slowly from the car. When I did not pull the door closed right away, he reached over and yanked it shut. He drove away from my building. He drove away from my curb and away from my life.

"Ty...please don't go," I heard myself pleading. I stepped out into the street and raised my hand as if to wave. I was crying uncontrollably. But, then I paused. I stood on the street, my hand partially raised, then let it drop by my side. I couldn't do it. I could not bring myself to try and stop him.

The car suddenly lurched to a stop and my heart jumped. Had he changed his mind? He reversed and halted beside me. The passenger side window came down. I looked in slowly.

"Ty," I whispered.

"I need my ring."

Twenty Seven

Sometimes it was all I thought about. Every word we spoke to each other. How had it fallen apart so quickly? It had been three weeks since we had broken up, and I still had not been able to join all of the broken pieces. Every day I wanted to call him. I wanted to beg him to forgive me, and tell him I did not love Quincy, and that he could trust me. I knew he still loved me. I still loved him, so why couldn't we make it work? But it occurred to me, that I hadn't spoken the words he had asked me to. I had faltered at the worst possible time. I didn't know even now if I could say those words to him again. What I did know, however, was that I wanted him in my life. He was so good to me. I had to love him. Yet, I always came up with this empty feeling when I whispered the words to myself, pretending I was speaking to him. It hurt like hell to realize that.

Seventeen times in one day, I had picked up the phone to call him. He had asked me not to call. So technically I couldn't call. Over the next few days I wallowed in my sorrow at night. I tried to avoid Quincy. I went to work. I went to see my mother. I went to the gym. Nothing seemed the same to me anymore. Sometimes I cried because I missed him. Sometimes I laughed because I had really managed to screw it up. I screwed it well, too.

One day, while Quincy was out job hunting I lay on the couch, crying so hard my chest began to hurt. My nose ran, and my eyes were raw. I felt awful, but I could not bring myself to stop thinking about him. At the exact moment when I was begging God to take me away from my misery, there was a loud banging on my door. I held my breath. Was it God? The loud bang came again. I sat up, concerned. Why didn't they just assume I wasn't home? It was probably someone from down the hall. The urgent banging came again. I went to the peephole. After looking out, I hung my head in shame. When I opened the door all the girls, led by my mother, stared at me. My mother pulled me into her arms and hugged me. I sobbed, certain I would run out of tears.

There were still pictures of him all over my apartment that I could not bring myself to take down. I wished every time my phone rang, that it would be him. I wished that he would just show up at my door. Every time I saw my dog Sammy, he reminded me of Ty. I wondered if I would have to get rid of Sammy because my heart was breaking. My sheets still smelled of him. I found a bottle of his cologne and his deodorant in my bathroom. His bathrobe that I gave him for Christmas was still hanging behind my bathroom door. I couldn't get him off my mind. I remembered the way he had made me feel about myself. I loved the romantic things he did for me. I loved his laugh. I loved the thickness of his body. I missed the way his voice sounded when we spoke late into the night. I loved the little spot on the side of his nose that wrinkled when he was perplexed. I loved the ticklish place behind his knees. I loved the way our bodies seemed to fit together. How could he just leave me like that? How dare he? The problem, I realized, was because he had formulated some sort of mold for me. He thought I was perfect. I wasn't. I never claimed to be perfect.

❤❤❤

"Is this him?" Quincy asked, picking up a photo of Ty that was sitting on my dresser. Quincy had been at my house for almost two months now.

"Yes," I replied, and grabbed my shoes.

I slipped my feet into my heels and then stood in the mirror fixing my hair.

He sat on my bed watching me. "You look nice," he said.

"You know what, Quincy?" I said. "So do you. Ever since you were released, you look so different."

"Getting out of jail does that to you." He chuckled.

I swept my hair off my shoulders to put up into a bun. He coughed, and I turned around to look at him. "What?"

"Looks better down with that outfit," he whispered. I piled it up on top of my head anyway. I was going to work, not a beauty contest.

"What are you doing today?" I asked him.

On the day he was released, my mother and I went with him to Central Park. We ate hot dogs, ice cream and talked for hours. Then we went to my mother's place to gather his things, which was where they were being stored. Despite that he was no longer in jail, he still wasn't a free man. He had a lot of paperwork to go through. Marcus was talking about suing the NYPD. We had to go to the courthouse, social security, income tax, and to the doctor's office. There was a lot a man had to do after being released from jail.

"Going to your mother's place. Then to Aunt Ruth's. Then I'm gonna go and look for a job," he replied.

That sounded like a great day. I had been moderately worried that he might get back to his old tricks. But, things seemed to have changed.

"Will you be here for dinner?" I asked.

"Well, seeing how I'll have to cook it, I suppose."

"You know what, Quincy, I am not that bad a cook." I laughed, with a bobby pin stuck in my mouth. I turned around to glare at him.

"Not if you like fried peanut butter, and microwaved chicken."

"You're not even funny," I snapped. "Can you make some coffee, please?"

"Sure thing!"

He left my room. I sighed. Things were perfect, with the exception of one thing. I missed Ty like a son-of-a-bitch. I had to admit that I wasn't completely over the urges to call him.

❤❤❤

When I got home that evening, there was gangster rap blaring on the CD player. I kicked off my shoes, unbuttoned my jacket and flopped down on the couch with my mail. Good-bye Donnell and D'Angelo. It was nice knowin' ya. Poor Sammy had been yapping at my feet when I walked in the door, but I hadn't even heard him over the music.

"You poor thing," I said, and scooped him up into my arms. He was so damn cute, I kissed his nose, and he looked at me with those wide, brown puppy dog eyes. I put him on my stomach, as usual, and leaned my head back on the couch to read the mail.

"Hi!" I called, remembering I wasn't here alone. I reached over to the remote to turn down the music. It was too loud for my baby Sammy for sure.

"Are you home already?" Quincy asked, and came out of the kitchen. He leaned over the couch to stroke Sammy's fur.

"The usual time."

"The NYPD decided to make a deal. And it's got about five figures in it."

"Lie!" I yelled.

"No. Marcus called fifteen minutes ago. They don't want to be sued. They wanna try and keep this from further going to press, too," he said.

"Holy shit, Quincy. Do you realize the implication of this?" I squealed.

"This means that I have enough money to start anything I please. I can go anywhere I choose. And pay you back for getting me Marcus," he said, with a fantastic smile.

"You don't have to do that. You would have done the same for me," I told him.

"I will!" he said, and I knew there would be no room for argument.

Over dinner, he looked up at me for what seemed like ages.

"What?"

"Did you read the letter?" he asked. His eyes met mine squarely.

"This is fabulous. What is it?" I asked, pushing a piece of my fish around in the sauce. I looked down at my plate. I didn't want to talk about it. I was hoping he might have forgotten about it. I had tried to forget about it.

"Coquille St. Jacques," he replied. "Just say so, if you didn't."

"No!" I said softly.

"Good!"

"Good, why?" I asked, alarmed.

"Because I want it back! Just give it to me, and I won't mention it again." He stuck his fork in his mouth.

"Why?" I asked feeling hurt, but trying not to show it.

"Because, it was silly to give it to you. In fact I am quite embarrassed about it. I think it's just because I was in the pen and feeling sappy and what not. I don't think I really meant it." He reached under the table. I knew that he was petting Sammy.

"Why would you say that?" I asked him. I was perturbed, upset. I wanted the note.

"Because it was impulsive and stupid. What's your problem? You're in love with that guy," he retorted.

I dropped my fork on my plate. "So it *was* about love?"

"You know what it was about!" he snapped. He looked up at me again, frustrated, but with remorse in his eyes. "I'm sorry."

"I can't give it back!" I exclaimed.

"Why not?"

"Because…because. I just can't!" I replied.

I was huffing and puffing. I had to stand up, because my stomach was turning over. I felt like vomiting. I walked to the fridge, and stuck my head in it. I know how stupid that must have looked, but it was the first thing that came to mind.

When I came out, he looked at me puzzled. "You're playing games," he said. He had turned around in his chair, so he could look directly at me. It was a challenging look.

"I don't play games."

"That's what they all say. I'm telling you, you don't need to see it. This note will set the ball rolling. The ball is still in my court… if you give the note back to me."

"You've changed your mind then?"

"Yes!" he said, too quickly.

"No!" I said softly. "You haven't."

He frowned, leaned back and straightened the folds in his dress pants. "It all seems like it might have been a dream to me. Like I haven't spent the last year locked behind bars. That two years ago, I wasn't doing break and enters, getting high, doing nothing with my life. And then I was forced to sit down, with my thoughts, my feelings, and just think. I found that all the confusion that cluttered my mind, was not completely confusion. That I just needed to sort them out. With pen and paper. I leave my soul on paper. I leave my heart. Now I realize that what I wrote in that note, is more than words; it's too much for anyone to see." When he was done he looked up at me.

"You don't think I can handle it?" I asked. Then, I felt I understood better why Ty had been so upset. I had not yet read the note, but if Quincy had been that honest, it would definitely be a shock to Ty.

"I don't think it's fair!" he replied.

"I don't think I could give it back if I wanted to," I whispered, and turned away. And then it hit me. How had I disassociated my first sexual experience and the importance of it, from the actual person that I did it with. That was Quincy. You don't forget about those things. Ever! You always feel something for them. Did we have unfinished feelings? He had been so tender and so gentle with me. It was so easy to care for someone who cared completely for you. It was just us. No years of relationships, or broken marriage proposals was going to take those feelings from me. Especially if there were unfinished things between us.

"I need time. But I promise to let you know what happens," I said finally.

Then I stopped. I knew what the answer was. God was there moving boxes in my mind. He had found some space for me to move around freely. There was a lot less clutter in my head. I knew then what the answer was. I knew then, what the answer had always been.

Twenty Eight

The time I needed was three months. I received a promotion. I was so shocked about that. I had missed work for various reasons. There was the time during the trial, my mother's surgery, Miss Dee's death, and after Ty and I had broken up. I felt like I had been a rocket, exploding from one minute to the next. When Ron called me into his office in mid October, I was certain I was going to be fired.

"Tamara, how are things over in finance today?" he asked, with a smile. He sat down at his desk at the same time I sat in the chair opposite him.

"Stellar!" I replied. "As usual."

"Tori still making mistakes?" he asked.

"Tori's getting better," I responded. I didn't mention the loss of three very important faxes by her the week before, which had taken me almost six hours after work to track down. No, he didn't need to know that.

"Good!" He leaned back in his chair and crossed his arms. Right behind him, the sun played light games in his dark hair. He really was a handsome man for his age. He stood about six feet two, with broad shoulders and jet-black hair.

"I have a proposal," he said, and that was when my heart skipped a beat. He was going to propose I move down to some lower-paying job. This was it! I had worked like a dog to get things back to normal as fast as possible, and now this!

"I know there have been tragedies like crazy in your life, these last few months." I nodded solemnly. "I was impressed!"

"Impressed?" I asked, my eyes widening.

"Yes!" he replied. "First, the only person here who knew about them was me. Meaning, you didn't let it interfere with your work. Second, you pulled everything together, right away, once you returned. That takes perseverance. Third, I've seen people fall apart at the seams, with just one of the problems you've had! You didn't. You have the dedication, and drive to survive at Bronx West." I was incredibly embarrassed at all the glory he was placing on me. I nodded, still wide-eyed.

"I need an assistant. Right-hand person, if you wish! Partner in crime, learning the tricks of the trade. I'm about ready to kick the bucket myself. I have one foot in the grave, Tamara. The only person I can see running this place is a Miss Tamara Jones. So if you will accept the promotion, the job is yours."

"I'll accept!" I said the minute he was done. The raise in salary would be off the wall. Yes! Of course I would bloody well accept.

He sat back in his chair smiling, a look of satisfaction on his face.

That had been in October. And almost immediately, they had Janine, the head employee in my previous department, trained for my job. In no time at all, I was at cocktail parties, and dinners, schmoozing with the likes of Cameron Diaz's agent. Once we had dinner with Sally Field. We met Jessica Simpson's agent, and her father, to discuss the budget for a new film. At first I thought I would be getting coffee for him, and typing or printing his messages, but he had a secretary for that. I was his right-hand woman. I went places with him. He taught me the art of canoodling. Meaning how the hell to get what the hell you wanted out of people without making them feel hella cheated or intimidated. He had the skills.

My mother, Quincy and I celebrated with a barbecue on my mother's back porch. And then later I met the girls for drinks at The Apple.

"We need to sort something out," Traci piped up. "Christmas Eve, we had a brawl. I mean a real crazy brawl. Because of Tamara's break-up, we all pulled together again. But, I still feel the tension in here. I want everything out on the table. We need a circle of trust. No one can leave here pissed off or mad. So, you hussies better think about what you're saying before you say it."

"I don't have anything to say," Jaclyn said. "I had a crazy past. I admit that. But, my life is different now. God's light is shining on me. I know that it is hard to adjust. You only know me as the old Jaclyn. But, here I am sipping my orange juice instead of liquor. I am already succeeding."

I admired Jaclyn. My mother had always led me toward a path of righteousness. Jaclyn had not had that. Her journey seemed so much longer and more painful than mine. Yet, here she was standing up for everything she had recently come to believe. She had made the transition in such a short time. My heart swelled with pride for her.

"We appreciate it," I said to her. I put my hand on hers. "We will all be changed for the better." She nodded and looked at the rest of them, who also nodded.

"I'm leaving," Daeshondra piped in. "Teaching is just not cutting it for me. I cannot live in my mother's house any longer. I feel as though there is something I need to do for the greater good. I'm going to Nairobi. I'm going to volunteer in a poor community in Nairobi."

"What?" Olivia asked.

We echoed her. "When?"

"In two months," Daeshondra replied and I felt that sinking feeling in the pit of my stomach. I was sad.

"Are you sure this is what is right for you?" Precious asked her.

"It is just something I have to do. I don't know for how long. But, I know where." For a moment there was silence.

Then I said, "If that is what you think you should do, then that is where you should go."

"Well…I know you guys couldn't get ahold of me. I lost the baby. I've been seeing a shrink. I needed to get help with the… you know. The pills," Shan whispered. Devora rubbed her back and smiled at her.

"We are here for you. Even Dae in Nairobi," she said and we laughed.

Devora had signed the divorce papers. She would be divorced in a few months. They had a prenup, so things would be relatively drama free. Traci announced that she was thinking about moving to Victoria, Canada. The Canadian artist she had been seeing for four years wanted to live with her. Olivia had filed for full custody of her son, so that her ex-boyfriend Brick could not have more than supervised visits. Precious was pregnant again, with twins.

"Let's not do this again!" I stated. "It was terrible. We are all too great to be divided."

We raised our glasses to that.

At one point I heard a very distinct, familiar laugh. It was Ty. I would know it anywhere. I looked in the direction the sound was coming from. There he was. He wasn't looking at me. If he had looked up he would have seen me staring at him. His eyes, however, were trained on his dinner date. He threw his head back and laughed, in that way that I had loved. I thought I might die.

For just a moment, I imagined it was me he was sitting with. I hadn't seen him in such a long time. I hadn't heard him laugh in what seemed like longer. As I stared at him, I thought of the red wine I could no longer drink, the foods I'd had to abandon, and the movies I could no longer watch. They were all things that reminded me of him, and our time together. They were like a particular fragrance that brought back the most graphic memories to you.

I wanted to go over and talk to him. But, something told me not to. I was supposed to be healing. The farthest I'd gotten, however, was to taking his clothes from my drawers, and putting them in a box. I would have to retrace all those steps if I went up to him now and he still rejected me. Furthermore, he was sitting there with a woman. Tall, with long legs, and long black hair, a weave for sure. She was wearing nice, expensive shoes I knew from the way they fit her feet. Maybe Prada. And, even though I couldn't see her face, I knew that she was beautiful. A pang of jealousy surged through my head, and then it remained. I didn't want to imagine him with someone else. I am not a jealous person. This is not a feeling that I might like to entertain. He reached across the table, and with his finger, caressed the line of her jaw. My chest felt as though a dagger had just been driven through it. I made a quiet, gagging sound. The girls didn't notice. I loved it when he touched me in delicate little places like that. Places like the joining of my two nostrils, or the web between my fingers, or the curve in my throat. I needed to leave. I stood up suddenly.

"Where are you going?" Shan asked.

I ignored her and grabbed my purse. I turned toward the rear of the restaurant, toward the restrooms. Once inside the restroom,

I felt as though I was gasping for the last breaths of air in the world. I grabbed the countertop to steady myself. I looked up into the mirror only to find that nothing had changed, except my haphazard posture. Another woman entered the room and looked at me. I stood up straight, and reached into my purse for my powder. I dabbed absentmindedly at my face.

"He's out there with another woman," I heard myself whisper. A voice in my head told me that he could do whatever he wanted. What did I need, separation papers? It wasn't like we were married and I had died or something!

I took two heaping breaths of air. I took my comb from my purse and ran it through my hair. I looked pretty. I was probably prettier than she was. He had no idea who I was. He hadn't even given me a chance to explain. And, besides, clearly there was a reason I hadn't told him everything. We were *never* meant to be. I had just wished for it.

I walked out of the restroom pretending to feel renewed. But, that was the last thing I felt.

When I got in, Quincy was on his way out. He was going to purchase a laptop, so he could write.

"Can you do me a favor when you get back?" I asked him.

"What's that?" he said from the doorway. He leaned down to scratch Sammy behind the ears.

"Take down all these damn pictures of that punk!" I said.

I heard him laughing as I walked down the hall to my room.

Twenty Nine

It was August, my birthday month. Quincy had gotten the Bantam contract. He was renting a condo in New Rochelle. It was a really nice condo, at that. He spent a lot of time writing. He talked of buying a cabin on a lake in Canada so he could get away to write. The Bantam contract started with five poems to publish in a book of poetry, for more money than he even dared to admit. He had been busy perfecting each poem.

From his fridge, I brought him a beer and myself an iced tea.

The man I visited in jail stood in front of me, but I no longer considered him the misguided troublemaker he used to be. He was a man with a future, with dreams and a lot of promises that I knew that he would keep.

"If airplane black boxes are supposedly indestructible, then why the hell don't they make the entire plane from that stuff?" I asked.

"Because then you'd have to drive the plane, not fly it," he replied sarcastically. I do believe that was the first time he had ever had an answer to one of my dumb questions.

Quincy was in a pair of khaki shorts, and a white muscle shirt. He looked amazing. Those muscles were screaming for some-one to touch them. I wore a tank top, and a jean skirt. We were both sitting on lawn chairs, watching Parys run around the yard.

I had taken her out for lunch and to the zoo. She busily chased a plastic bag around the yard.

"I miss her!" he said so softly that I almost didn't hear him.

"Who?" I asked absentmindedly.

"Miss Dee," he replied, looking up dreamily.

"We all do," I told him.

"I met my father once." He snickered. "He was a joke. I found his address in Miss Dee's phonebook, and went to find him. Just to see what he looked like. He lived in the ghetto. I'm talking Harlem, Tamara. With eight snot-nosed little kids. Some of them white, some of them black, running around the yard. I knew that he wasn't feeding or clothing any of them. Not one! He looked at me, as though he didn't know who I was. Then he called me the son of a whore. Said my mother kicked him out because he was cheating on her. He had the nerve to say, 'Look at me now.' Like he was livin' it up. I knew he was on something. Coke, heroin, I don't know. But I had to leave. Had to get away, because I might have hit him. But it was the worst feeling in the world. To see that was part of where I had come from. He had helped bring me into this world. I couldn't see what the hell my mother had ever seen in him," he said quietly. "I have never hated someone so much!"

"I'm sorry," I whispered. When I looked over there was a tear trickling down his cheek, as he looked up at the sky. I can't explain what it felt like to see him cry. Tough guys don't cry, unless something really hurts. Everything was hurting him. My heart went out to him. I got up off the chair to sit beside him, and hold his hand. He took it in his and turned it over and over. He had done that so often in the past. The last time I was still wearing Ty's engagement ring. I reached up with my right hand,

and brushed the tear away, but one fell down the other cheek, and then there was an entire series of them. He sat up, and I put my arms around him, and he put his around me. He cried on my shoulder. Before I knew what was happening, I was crying along with him. I could feel the rise and fall of his chest, as he heaved the pain out through his eyes. This wasn't a man crying for any reason other than to rid himself of years and years of pain.

"I...I...was s...so mad. How could she die? B...Before I could tell her I loved her so much. Th...that I was sorry? I need her. The last time she came, she kissed me extra long. It was like she knew. I felt so much from her at that moment, but being the man I was, I just pulled back. I acted like I was too old to be kissed by my mother." He cried noisily, his body shaking with pain.

I leaned back, untangled my arms from him, and brushed his tears aside. I placed one, two, three, four kisses, on his dark, wet cheek. There was something about those kisses. I knew that I would never kiss him the same way ever again. I felt as though there would be more kisses. But, these kisses possessed some special sort of magic.

"It felt sort of like...," I whispered. It was on the tip of my tongue. I could feel his emotions and his pain so acutely as we held each other.

"The last good kiss I would ever recieve."

We had both uttered the words at the exact same time. It was from a movie we had watched in a theater when we had dated so long ago. It seemed like another lifetime entirely. Yet, that line found us in the place we were in now. They were my thoughts, and they were his thoughts. I felt like asking if he was talking about my kiss, or his mother's. But, instead, I said nothing.

He looked up at me eyes wide, and then we embraced again.

There were no more kisses, and no more words, only the heat, and compassion from both our warm bodies soothing each other. I wanted to erase all the hurt and confusion. Turn the past into non-existent. But, I didn't have that power. I could only be around now.

"I'm here for you, Quincy. Always," I said, and even though he didn't stop crying, his sobbing subsided. His breathing sounded regular again, as he rested his head on my shoulder. Inside my head, I thanked God for *fixing everything*.

All of my senses were filled with Quincy. I felt that I loved him. There were no questions of confusion. I had no empty, curious feeling. He filled me up.

"It's like trying to unscramble scrambled eggs."

"Huh?" I looked at him confused.

"I was trying to explain how much I love you," he replied.

"So you used scrambled eggs as a metaphor?"

"It was the best I had."

Epilogue

Hi Baby,

I was thinking of you last night, even while you were sitting across the table from me. Thank you for blessing me with your love, your presence and your grace. My life is so complete with you and the twins in it. I can't imagine myself anywhere but with you at my side. Please never forget how much I love you. You're so sexy!

Your one and only husband

I find this note tucked away in the pocket of my favorite suit. I have no clue when he wrote this. That is besides the point. The point is that it has cut a long wide smile across my face, and made me think of my husband, and my kids. I lean back in my chair, just as Anita, my secretary, walks in with a stack of papers.

"Hi, Nita," I say cheerily. I fold the note, and put it in my pocket.

"You look like you just won a million dollars," she says, smiling.

"I hit the jackpot every day," I reply with a laugh. I know she knows I'm talking about my family.

"The old checks to sign, boss."

"Once these are ready to go out, why don't you take the afternoon off, Anita?"

"I love you, you know that?" she asks.

What can I say? I'm so happy. I'm right where I want to be. With who I want to be with.

Ron Sallinger retired four years ago, on my thirtieth birthday to be exact. He joked that it was a present for me. At the time, I had been his right hand for the past four years. Now I run Bronx West Global. I love it.

My mother is still going strong. I personally think that she and Trevor are dating. She won't tell me the truth. She claims she is too old for dating. I don't think you can ever be too old for romance, though. But, whatever it is they have, Trevor is a companion for my mother. I praise God every day for that.

Which brings me to Tyrone. He is engaged to a lawyer from Orange County. Not the same woman I first saw him with years ago. No, this one he met while on a business trip, somewhere in Europe. I don't see him often. Sometimes I run into him at my mother's house. We are civil to each other. It would be mighty awkward, if we couldn't be. We've never mentioned us. That suits me just fine. If he ever wants to have a closer friendship, I am definitely open to that. But it no longer hurts. I no longer think about what I may have missed or what I may have lost. It doesn't matter anymore. I wish him luck.

Devora never spoke to Bobby again. Because of their prenup, they parted without conflict. She recently got engaged to a doctor she met in Paris. He moved to New York, and she has decided to retire and manage an exclusive travel agency. She and I finally have the closeness we used to have back in primary school.

Daeshondra spent one year in Nairobi, then went to Sierra Leone, then Mozambique. In addition to overseas teaching, she is also an activist for AIDS awareness and education in Africa.

Jaclyn married David the preacher. We would never have thought she would be a preacher's wife. She quit modeling, and works for the church every day. Although her life is extremely different, the few times we do manage to meet, she shows up with bells on.

Olivia didn't end up getting anywhere near court. Her ex-boyfriend, the drug addict, who wanted custody, was scared away by her lawyer. Shortly after that, he ended up in jail for being drunk and disorderly. She bought a brand-new house, and started dating her real estate agent.

Precious is still with that no-good husband of hers and the rest of us speculate that she will never leave. She now has seven children, and swears that is it. She will no longer have anymore. None of us believe it. She has gone back to school. She is working toward a degree in computer programming.

Shan finally found the man of her dreams. He denied her for a loan, so she told him off. Shortly after that they went on their first date. A short six months later, they married. She finally made it to the altar, and has not looked back since.

Traci Williams is now Traci Bordeaux. She married her Canadian man. They moved out to what seems like the Canadian end of the world, British Columbia, but I've been up there to see her and her family twice. Jaclyn and I went right after she had their first little boy, Dorian. So now they have two children. Rochelle, from her old boyfriend back in high school, who is now seventeen, and pregnant. Not much you can do there, huh? Traci has continued to paint and is currently entertaining the thought of opening her own gallery in Victoria. I hope it all works out for her.

And of course you are wondering about Quincy Baker. My childhood friend. Well, he's now married, has two children: Margo and Daniel. He and his wife moved out to Queens, and bought a great big house out there. He got a book deal with Bantam, and has not only started a new poetry book, but has started writing short stories, and exploring the idea of doing a novel for them. He's been featured on the *Times* Best Newcomer list. He is ecstatic. He and his wife are happy. I am sure you have guessed by now, that I am his wife and we have our four-year-old twins and are enjoying life to the fullest.

So, it was always Quincy, wasn't it? The line that got me came on my twenty-eighth birthday. He had taken me to Pallisade's before I went out with the girls for the evening. At the end of the meal, he just said it; it popped out of his mouth , I guess.

"I have loved you all of my life, and Tamara, it's not going away." Then he looked up maybe a full ten seconds later to see the expression I had on my face. And finally I knew it was time, it was him. It was there in front of me all along, and I couldn't fight it anymore.

In the midst of all the attention and celebration at my wedding, I had sat down at the table with all of the girls. Devora was telling a story and everyone looked at her intently. Traci sat on one side of me, her hand resting absently, yet warmly on my arm. Jaclyn sat on the other side of me, so close to me, the fabric on my wedding dress had spilled over and onto her lap. The magic of the evening got me then. I looked around at them all, caught in a dreamlike state. The corners of my scene became cloudy. The music, and the beautiful mood lighting, cast a pleasant glow on the picture. Then I saw them. My mom and Trevor were on the dance floor. "Rock Me Tonight" by Freddie Jackson was playing. They moved slowly, but sure of themselves. Lost in each other, like I was lost in my dream. They danced. They danced like a couple that had been dancing for fifty years. I was certain she had found the love of her life.

Shortly after the wedding, we moved into a house with a big

backyard and a quiet street for our kids to play. Margo and Daniel were born the following year. Both of them look like spitting images of him. I got cheated in that sense, I guess. But my kids, my friends, my mother, my husband, my house, my dog Sammy are the light of my life.

Oh! And one more thing, if you haven't figured it out yet; there's a poem somewhere at the beginning of this book. It just happens to be the one that Quincy wrote to me while he was in jail, and then tried to take back. I finally read it, and decided that I wanted it forever printed in history. He was right; it was his soul right on paper. And now it's forever entwined with mine.

About the Author

Janice Pinnock enjoys traveling, sports, and reading. Janice currently lives in Canada, where she is working on her next novel. You may email the author at janicepinnock@gmail.com